T0147828

Rupert's Journey

»✶✶✶«

RUPERT MICHAEL

authorHOUSE®

AuthorHouse™
1663 Liberty Drive
Bloomington, IN 47403
www.authorhouse.com
Phone: 1-800-839-8640

First published by AuthorHouse   04/18/2011

ISBN: 978-1-4567-6038-0 (e)
ISBN: 978-1-4567-6039-7 (hc)
ISBN: 978-1-4567-6040-3 (sc)

Library of Congress Control Number: 2011905211

Printed in the United States of America

Contents

Foreword

Greetings, reader. My name is Rupert Michael, and this book recounts a most improbable journey I experienced a few years ago. It was not a journey of choice. In fact it was completely unexpected, and I resisted for much of the way. When the journey was over I came to realize that I should write it down, and that is how this book eventually came to be.

This experience has completely changed my life, giving me a perspective I didn't used to have, and opening my eyes to much which I had previously not realized. I believe the changes in me are for the better. I hope that after reading you will agree. I return to this account frequently to relive the adventure, which inspires me and reminds me of what is really important. I hope that you will also be entertained and inspired.

Best Regards,
Rupert Michael

Beep! Beep! Beep! Beep! I don't know how long it had been going before Sharon punched me in the ribs to indicate I need to shut the blasted alarm clock up.

Whack, I slap the button and drag myself out of bed.

Four in the morning – the price I pay for a huge house in the suburbs and two luxury vehicles. Well, Sharon does work a part-time job to help out.

I feel my way through the dark toward the shower.

Sharon is my wife. We've been married for five years. Everything is going well. I'm moving up in my job and making good money.

Pshhh, I turn on the shower and the cold water hits the enclosed floor.

It's a normal morning – up at four, to work by six, back home by eight, to bed by ten. Lather, rinse, repeat.

Ugh, the water is still cold. I hate standing every morning like this on the cold bathroom floor with my hand monitoring the chilly water until I can finally step into comfort. Ah, warmth at last.

I've been going like this for years, getting between four and six hours of sleep per night and working ten to twelve hours a day. My job is salaried – I'm not paid more for overtime – not directly at least. I simply can't afford to do anything less, or there will be no more promotions, or worse.

Lather, rinse, repeat... Does anyone repeat? Once seems like enough to me when I do it every day.

My commute is one to two hours depending on traffic. If there's rain or a wreck, forget it – I won't be home before ten.

Thump, I turn off the shower.

My employer doesn't provide covered parking so I use the public garage a half mile away and hike back and forth. With the criminals in the city, it's a certainty my car would otherwise be broken into. I'm not about to leave the investment of my vehicle out for them. I positively hate the city and I can't trust that kind of people.

Fwhoosh, I throw the towel back over the shower door and I've finally recovered my faculties.

To top off the parking situation, the public garage is marked for compact cars. That is so frustrating. I don't apologize for using two spaces. People should encourage buying domestic cars, not the cheap midget foreign junk.

I step out of the bathroom all dressed and ready to go. Raow! Stupid cat in the way again. I kick at it as it dashes away.

I hate cats, but the wife insists. I want a dog. A *big* dog. A real pet. A guard pet. But the wife refuses. She did point out to me that she would be the primary caregiver, and she said she's "not taking care of a huge, slobbering, butt-licking (and face-licking) dog."

"Besides," she said, "Fluffy could not co-exist, and I'm not giving up my cat." I don't like it one bit, but I have to agree with her. At least for now.

Sharon is always asleep when I head out to work. She usually goes to work herself about eight or nine, and sometimes in the afternoon.

Thwock, I unlock the front door and head out.

I have to lock the door with a key as if it's the Stone Age because my car doesn't fit in the garage. They make garages so small to force me to drive a tinny small car. No way I'm doing that. I make good use of the remote start on cold days, you better believe it.

Ah, my car – plenty of elbow room. Above the fray, the rest of you rabble better keep your distance.

I enter the car and push the start button. Vroom… Ding! Ugh, got to fill up already.

What a cruel joke it is that it costs so much to keep gas in the tank. The stupid tank is too small.

Off I go on the long, long drive to work.

Oh, how I hate the gas companies conspiring to jack up the prices. I can't make it very far on this low of a tank, so I've got to first stop at the local station. The needle is below empty by the time I finally pull up to the pump.

I need an in-flight refill. As I watch the numbers on the pump turn to tell my doom, I begin to fantasize about hooking up to a tanker on the fly down the highway, and clunk! the tank is all filled up.

Another eighty bucks to the oil company profits. How do they get away with making so much money off of us? They could easily get by at a much lower price. Well, at least this isn't a boycott day. Then I would be in real trouble.

I like to listen to talk-radio in the car. Every morning I have to shake my head in dismay at the stories of the moronic things that people do.

I merge onto the highway, and, as usual, within a few miles it's bumper-to-bumper all the way into the city. The stories about the ridiculous behavior by foreigners always make me chuckle. This morning there's one about some guy from India who conducts electricity through himself to power a light bulb. Why do foreigners waste all their time on such stupidity?

I finally make it to downtown. Whaaaa! I slam the horn at the midget foreign car driving entirely too slow in the lane I need to be in. He tries to speed up just as I try to pass him, and I just make it to the entrance of the public garage, tires squealing.

Look what the moron made me do. Your little junk car has no power, loser. I rush around to the top level where I can find open spaces, and some truck has taken two spaces and left one and a half, the only space in the whole structure where I can fit my car. I back mine deftly into the opening and jump out.

Thunk! My door knocks into the foreign car next to me. No damage to mine, no problem.

》＊＊＊《

I finally reach my cube at six – faster than normal, considering the pit-stop. I can be home early today. Dee-doo! As soon as I log in I've Got Mail. My inbox is already overflowing. I process the first email, and by the time I lift my head it's ten-thirty.

I hate to hear the senseless ranting of my neighbor about the government. "If you hate this country so much, why don't you just leave and see how you like it over there," I picture myself replying. If I only had a walled office, I wouldn't have to tolerate such annoyances. I should have had it years ago.

Dee-doo! More mail. Ugh, back to work. Next thing I know it's twelve-thirty, and my "fat-ass obnoxious neighbor," as I privately refer to him, is inviting me to lunch again.

"Brought lunch today," I reply courteously, and he walks away.

I don't know why they haven't fired the guy already, wasting an hour at lunch while I don't miss a beat. If I don't get the walled office before him, I'll have to look for another job. I sure can't afford to be unemployed, though. I already take the payout for my unused vacation days to keep the credit cards from getting out of control. I down the lunch Sharon packed for me while continuing to process the emails.

Dee-doo! The mail never stops. I'll have to process it on the phone, because I have a meeting to go to.

»＊＊＊«

It seems I paid no attention in that meeting, because I have no memory of it now.

One meeting down, off to another, and the next thing I know it's five-thirty and the boss just headed out. By six I'm out the door myself with an hour or two of commute between me and dinner. Sweet. I'll be home early tonight.

I dash into the elevator, and boong, boong, boong, on down the floors it goes, but not nearly fast enough. I push through the crowds of people just loitering in the lobby and wasting my time, and hustle the couple of blocks back to the parking garage. I see the traffic all around is standing still from the congestion, as usual.

I make it to the garage and find no revenge marks on my door. Vroom! I start all eight cylinders and get in the long line of cars toward the exit. It's probably twenty minutes getting out to the street, as the line merges into the stagnant traffic.

Whaaaa! I honk at yet another of the foreign midget cars in my way. Why would anyone drive a cheap small car when you can get a real one? So what if it costs more – you get more and you keep the money in your own country. You don't deserve to live here if you don't understand *that*.

I listen to more talk-radio on the long drive back home. It's a good thing we have people in the country to call it like it is. There's a presidential candidate on this evening.

"As President I will appeal any attempts by the Congress to raise taxes," he affirms. You'd better! Taxes are killing me!

"As President, I will make all current tax cuts permanent by law. Your hard-earned money will not be taken from you." That's what I want to hear.

"As President I will double military spending. We cannot let our enemies get the upper hand in this dangerous world. We will attack them before they attack us!" Amen, brother! Can't spend too much to keep us safe.

Click-click, click-click, click-click, click-click, the turn signal awaits my exit.

The candidate continues. "As President I will secure our borders. I have a plan to build a wall along every inch of our borders with foreign nations. They have proven they can't be trusted to keep our enemies out." Yes, please. Some neighbors we have. We have been too accepting of foreigners for too long.

I finally drive up to the front curb at home, fish the front door key out of my pocket, and make it back into the house.

Sharon is waiting with dinner. "You're late again." I look at my watch and realize it's a quarter after.

"Traffic."

"We should live closer to work," she replies, not for the first time.

Oh, how that annoys me. Work will have to move to me. I'm not living in the city, no way. I don't want to even look at her as we eat. It's always difficult for me to deal with her when I got worked up over politics. She is like so many other people, falling into a trap of complacence with enemies all around her. She's lucky she has a husband who's paying attention.

In a few minutes my favorite pundit is coming on. Shwooshhh, the water runs in the sink as Sharon cleans the dishes. I slide mine in without attempting to look at her.

Click, I turn on the television.

Without some common-sense logic every night I would go crazy with all the people out there that hate their own country. I just can't stand that. Politics are a sticking point between Sharon and me, and she's learned not to bring it up. It's always so frustrating trying to make her see the light, anyway.

"They're conditioning our children to be tolerant of homosexuality," the host states. "Unbelievable," I say and shake my head. We can't let these people take over the country.

Shhhwoop, the sink goes off and Sharon walks by into the bedroom without a word. I guess I'll have no luck with her tonight.

The host then has a nice piece about the same presidential candidate I was listening to earlier. It's a good thing we have media outlets that support the best candidate instead of trying to tear him down. We must have a strong President, not the weaklings who want to share the world with people who want to kill us. How can anyone support such a concept? Just get out and go live with them! Don't mind our bombs falling on your head!

Next thing I know the show is over and my mind is racing with anger over the state of the world. Click, I turn off the television.

We should stop having elections. People are too stupid to know what's best for them.

I shut off the lights and slip into my cold side of the bed and try to get to sleep. I keep going over in my head all the things that are conspiring against me, Sharon not the least.

I don't know what time it was when I got to sleep, but it was probably sometime before midnight.

02............   *A New Morning*

I awake to light. Morning already? Uh, morning! What time is it? I've gone and slept through the alarm! I can't be late to work!

I look to my side for the alarm clock, but it isn't there. I realize I'm not even in my bed. I'm lying on the floor. As I lay groggy and confused over my situation, I realize that yesterday was Friday.

Ah, that's a relief. I'm off this weekend. But where am I? Am I dreaming?

I look around me again. No, I'm quite obviously lying on the floor.

I realize the floor is a very deep pile carpet. That's odd. As my senses come to me I notice a wall in the distance — at least twenty feet away. My vision becomes clear — very clear, in fact. I can't recall having seen so clearly.

Where could I be that is so large a space?

Even though this carpet is strangely deep and thick, I'm sure it's an indoor carpet. I look back to the wall. It has a white moulding like an interior wall.

I realize that though I'm certain the wall is twenty feet distant, the moulding is so large that it must be very close.

Am I hallucinating? I don't remember drinking anything last night. Have I been drugged? I feel on the verge of panicking, but my curiosity at the strange surroundings is keeping my mind too occupied to lose control.

I look above me. Just over my head is an overhang. Along the edge is a large horizontal beam of wood. I turn to the right to see a pillar of the same dark wood about the same distance from me as the strange wall. Another beam stretches to the right above the pillar, which forms the corner of the structure above me.

It's darker underneath, but I can see another wall directly behind this beam. I now realize that the moulding of the wall is very large, at least two feet high.

Everything is massive here... I turn around to see two more pillars much further away supporting a rectangular-shaped ceiling above me. This ceiling is deeply recessed inside the broad pillars and covered in a heavy white cloth under smaller crossing beams.

What *is* this thing? It must be a pavilion of some sort, but like nothing I've ever seen. It's adjacent to one wall, but open to the other three sides. The beams are about four feet above the floor.

Why would anyone make a pavilion so low that an adult can barely sit up under it without hitting their head? Why is it made of such large beams of wood? It must have cost a fortune! Wait, what am I saying? This is crazy. I *must* be dreaming!

There is nothing inside – just the deep carpet. What is the purpose of all of this? Is it abandoned? Why is everything so large? It looks like this pavilion is within a larger indoor structure. But, what am I doing here anyway? How did I get here? What is this place?

Thump… Thump… Thump… I hear a dull throbbing noise. Thump… Thump… Thump! I can tell it's coming from the opposite side of the pavilion from the one I awoke facing.

I look in that direction and notice that it's much more open out from that side. I decide to waddle my way over to have a better look. I find that I can crawl on all fours, and quite nimbly.

It feels like walking, to tell the truth. Now that's odd.

Well, no, it's not odd at all, a voice in my head says. I have always walked on all fours. What other way is there? Walk on just the fore- or hind-legs? Absurd.

What? What did I say? I am definitely out of my mind!

I continue over to the other side and peek out from under the pavilion. The left adjacent wall stretches out to a far-away opposite wall. There is a great opening where the two walls should meet.

I look up to try to see how high the opening goes, when, Thump! Thump! Thump! A giant, at least forty feet tall, comes lumbering into the opening!

It's a doorway! I'm in a house of giants!

I stand frozen in terror as the giant approaches. It stops before me and begins to reach down a hand toward me. It actually seems friendly. I can tell it's a female giant. It vaguely resembles Sharon actually, but I'm too terrified to focus well enough, and a face looks very coarse when it's that huge.

As the hand gets closer, I leap backward under the pavilion. Or, as I begin to realize, it's a *bed*! Yes, I'm under a giant's bed!

Then a thought comes to my mind – yes, of course, I've always slept under here. Where else would I sleep? They are the masters. What? Did I say that?

I try to gather my wits while the giant still stands there. I look down at her massive feet. She wears socks that look like Sharon's.

I hear her mumble some rumbling sounds, and then she slowly turns and blunders back out the doorway.

What in the world? I go to sleep and wake up in a house of giants? Giants aren't real! What is wrong with me?

Still, I'm sure this can't be a dream. I've certainly never debated with myself whether I was dreaming while actually within a dream. No, this is definitely real!

I decide I have to have a look around and develop a plan for what to do. I watch out carefully for the giant, and crawl out of the pavilion on the side furthest from the door. I stand in the open floor. I can see gigantic dresser-drawers, and a huge set of white doors.

Is this *my* house? It's difficult to judge from this perspective, but it looks similar to the configuration of our master bedroom. I look back to what I had thought a pavilion before. I suppose it could very well be our bed.

I might as well stand now. What? I'm already standing? How did I go from crawling to standing?

"Never mind, I've clearly lost my brain," I say out-loud.

But, something else came out. My voice didn't speak those words. I spoke in some kind of strange rolling language.

What's next? I've got to figure out what the heck is going on here.

I look at the white doors. They are in the same position as the bathroom doors in our master bedroom, and look similar. I creep over to the doors, continuing to keep a close watch out for the giant. I notice that the doors are open enough to walk through.

I walk through the gap. The floor is covered with massive tiles, much like in our bathroom. I see a vast shower with glass walls to my right.

Yes, that looks the same I suppose. Beside that is a gigantic white tub. That could be ours too. To my left is another door that is closed. Behind that would be the toilet. A ledge far above runs along that wall with huge cabinet doors down to the floor. That would be the sink.

This must be my house! On the far side is a sliding mirror door that is opened to the left. I'm standing in line with the opening. I walk up and look inside.

Yep, the closet. The configuration is identical. The clothes stretch far, far above me, but they look familiar now that I'm wrapping my brain around the situation. There is a giant hamper just like mine.

I try to make sense of the state I'm in. I'm definitely awake. I'm definitely sober. Either this is my house, or it's a giant replica of my house.

Did I really see Sharon towering over me? Am I shrunken? How can this be real?

I turn back and remember the sliding door mirrors that stretch to the floor. I decide it would be interesting to see how I look in such an environment and I step before the mirror.

03..............   *An Improbable Discovery*

Staring at me is a giant house cat! A grey cat with black stripes, a white chin, and black paws. I start at first, thinking I'm about to be mauled, but I quickly realize this is a reflection of – *me*.

It's not a giant cat – it's more like I'm the size of a cat. Yes… I am… A cat. No! I'm not a cat! I pause and think that this cat looks familiar, but at that very moment I feel my brain overwhelmed with recollection pouring in. Ouch! Oww…

»✳✳✳«

Yes, I *am* a cat! Of course! What had gotten into my head before? What a silly cat I am. How did I get in here? I feel dizzy.

Just then I faintly hear the slow calling of my master. Yes, she is calling. What does she want now? Wait… That sounds familiar. This might be worth my time.

I quickly run out of the bathroom and make my way toward the voice. I can now distinctly hear her calling that she has food for me.

Yes! I run on toward the kitchen. She stands over a bowl that waits for me.

Waah, milk! My favorite! I hungrily begin lapping it up and she strokes my back.

Ugh, I hate it when she touches me when I'm eating. Do you have no manners at all? I arch my back and wave my tail, and she begins to get the message.

As I continue lapping up the milk, she blunders off. What do I care? She knows who really runs the place. Ahh, this is what it's all about. Milk is soooo delicious.

Once I finish I determine it's time to do some exploring. I walk to the back door.

Where has that stupid master gone off to? Don't you know it's my exploring time now? I wait for a while. Where is she? "Hey!" I call. "Hey!"

04............. A Day in the Life, Part 1

The master finally comes blundering over to the back door. She starts mumbling something to me in her language.

Yeah, yeah, whatever. Let me out already! I press my head into the slowly cracking gap until I finally burst out.

Ah, freedom! ... So, what to do? I don't see any butterflies or anything else interesting to play with. I decide to prowl over to the garden.

Yes, the masters grow some plants out here, for what reason I have no idea. The things are a ghastly mixture of colors and sizes. The biggest one has giant fruits growing from it.

Once I pulled one off and had a small taste of it, but bleh! those things are nasty. I was sick for days. Nope, not much to see here.

I decide to take a stroll around the yard. Wait, I see something moving nearby. Yes, some black bug is hopping through the grass.

Ah, the hunt is on! I crouch into attack position and deftly approach the vermin.

Closer, closer, Uh! The thing can jump quite far! This is great sport! Closer, closer, closer... Gotcha!

Ack! Wait, where is the bugger? I surely had it in my claws. There it is. You are a goner, pal.

Closer, closer, closer... Gotcha! Ugh, it got away again?

I look around for the critter, but I can't see it. I decide those are too hard to catch in the grass and stop looking. I return to my original plan to prowl the perimeter.

Ooh! There is a bird up in the tree! Aw, those things always keep so far away! I would dearly love to get my claws on that. I'll just have to wait for an opportunity.

Once I got up that pole in the garden and caught a bird. Yes, for some reason the masters actually built a home for birds there. They stuck a pole in the middle of the garden, and high up it they attached wooden boxes with holes in them so the birds could fit inside. Sometimes birds nest in there, and sometimes they perch on top of the boxes.

That one time I saw a bird fly to and fro from a box to a tree across the way. He just kept going back and forth. So, I climbed up behind the box and hung there waiting. Sure enough, the bird came flying back and I caught him! Ah, what a royal gift for the masters that was!

»✳✳✳«

Still, it is quite a lot of work to climb up that pole. There must be something else to do. Besides, the masters don't seem to like it when I try to catch birds.

Once she came out and grabbed me when I tried to climb the pole. She wouldn't let me outside the rest of that day.

I just don't understand them sometimes. I provide them gifts to earn my keep, but they don't always appreciate it. I thought they put those birdhouses up so I could catch birds for them. Oh, well.

I continue along the perimeter, and then I notice something that catches my eye near the far fence in the distance. Some creature is moving over there.

I rise up to have a good look, and... Yes, I can see it! It's a rat! A big one! Uh! It saw me! It's getting away!

I sprint after the thing as it shoots for the gap under the back fence. I've got you... Just on him, Gotcha! Ugh! It went under the fence.

I reach under the gap and paw for it, but he got away. I'll get you next time!

Hmm, what to do now? I decide to go to the front yard. I walk over to the gate. It looks closed. I reach out and pull at it, and, it's not locked! I pull the gate open and slip through. I rapidly survey the area, but don't see anything happening.

Sometimes rabbits can be found in this area. I saw one once that was half as big as me! But those things are *so* fast! I haven't caught one yet. But I will!

I walk around to the front yard. Birds are flying everywhere. Yes, birds, birds everywhere, and not a bite to eat!

I continue walking. It's very quiet, except... The big white thing in front of the yard is making a knocking noise.

Now what does that remind me of? Ah, yes! That means warmth! The huge thing is very warm underneath sometimes and makes strange noises, but it never moves.

I run under it and roll myself up in warm comfort. Ahh… This is a fine place for a nap…

Wait, I smell something. Oh no, it's… Dog. Ugh, yes, I smell dog. Well, I don't see it. I shuffle around and look in the reverse direction. Uh! There it is! It's tethered to its master.

Ugh, that is the biggest, ugliest mutt I've ever seen! Oh no! The beast sensed me! It's bellowing and dragging its master toward me! What do I do?

I bolt out from under the shelter and try to run back through the gate into the back yard. The dog roars. I run up to the gate, but the wind has blown it shut! I frantically try to claw up over it, but no use.

Uh! It'll see me! What do I do? I dart over behind a big metal box on the ground beside the house. After a time I can hear the dog passing on. Its master must have kept it out of the yard somehow.

Whew! I'm shivering. It's too cold. I move cautiously back toward the front yard, when the metal box I was behind begins making an awful noise that shoots right to my frayed nerves and I bolt back toward the big white thing I had slept under. Thankfully the dog isn't in sight now.

It's too cold out here. I'll go back inside. I walk up to the front door. I push on it. Locked again.

Why do the masters constantly interfere with me? I call for her. I sit and wait. Where is she? Hurry up already!

"Hey, I'm out here!" I call. "Let me in, now!" I wait. And wait. And wait.

It's so cold! I contemplate going back under the big white shelter. Yes, anything to keep warm. I walk back under it, but it's quiet now and not as warm as before.

Well, it's better than waiting exposed. I keep a look out at the door in case the masters finally come to let me in.

Oooooahh, I yawn. Might as well lay my head down while I watch out…

»*✳*«

The next thing I know the entire world is exploding around me! I wake up dazed and confused.

What's happening? The ground isn't even moving, but my ears are pounding!

Suddenly the giant thing over me begins to move! It's alive!

I don't budge, afraid it will step on me, and I close my eyes. The horrid sound passes on, and I open my eyes to see the beast rumbling away.

That was close! I run back to the door. I notice that it is now growing dark. The masters are still not coming.

Where is she? "Hey! Let me in!" I yell. It's too dangerous out here! Why do I have to depend on these stupid masters?

I hear a faint noise coming from within. Could it be? Yes! She has finally come!

Again, I burst through the door as soon as I can fit. I run to the kitchen. What, no food? The nerve! Are they trying to starve me?

I decide to take a look around. The master follows me in and starts trying to talk to me again.

Blah, blah. Whatever!

I decide to head back to the bedroom. I walk under the bed.

Hey, what is that? It's a mouse! I get into attack position…

Uh! No time! He's trying to escape! I dash after him. He scampers behind the bed. I fly around after him. I see him disappearing into the hole in the wall. I try to hook his tail, but he gets away.

I was so close. What a rare opportunity! Usually the masters call me when a mouse is sighted. I know they like it when I catch mice.

I'm so hungry. Wait, I smell something… Ooh, it smells fantastic!

I rush back to the door.

Oh, yes – I know that smell! I run into the kitchen, and the master is standing there over a bowl again.

Waah, tuna! My favorite! I dig in.

Again, she's talking to me. Why can't you give a cat some peace so it can eat? And don't you dare try to touch me!

She finally moves away and I finish the glorious meal. I strut into the living room licking my lips. I realize my claws could use some sharpening. Yes, the couch will do nicely. I walk over to it and the beastly master grabs me and starts talking to me again.

"Let me go!" I yell. My claws need sharpening! I'll use them on you!

I realize the master has seated herself and has opened that strange window. Somehow the masters open the window without touching it. They point at it with something in their hand and it suddenly opens. She strokes my back.

Hey, don't mess with me!

Somehow there's always something going on outside that window, but the colors are odd. She strokes my back again.

Ahh, that feels good…

It might be daytime out that window when it's night out the others. She strokes my back again.

Ahh, losing control…

That window is never cold, but sometimes a little warm. I tried to jump out of it a couple of times, but somehow I just bounced off. It's very noisy outside it when it's open. Sometimes I hear other cats or dogs. The masters will look through it for hours and hours, and sometimes they laugh at it. Crazy masters.

She strokes my back again.

Ooh, I'd like to take another nap. Ahh…

》＊＊＊《

I wake up. I'm lying on the couch. It's now completely dark.

The strange window must be closed again. It's completely black when it's closed. The masters have gone to sleep.

I jump down and head over to the kitchen.

No, of course there won't be any food left for me now that they've gone to sleep. Nope, not even an emptied bowl to lick.

I yawn and stretch. I might as well join them. It has been a long day.

I start to walk toward the bedroom, when I hear Kreeeeek! Kreeeeek! Kreeeeek! behind me. Hmm, I know that sound. I suddenly feel a bit more energetic.

I've caught one of these things before. They're fun to play with, even if you're not in a killing mood. In fact, I tried to catch one earlier today in the back yard.

Yeah, let's go have a look. I can see pretty well in the dark. I'll have a better chance to catch one on the bare floor.

I prowl around where I heard the noise, but I can't sense anything. I catch myself yawning again.

Yeah, it has been a long day. Let's just go to sleep.

I head toward the bedroom again, and am almost there when I hear Kreeeeek! Kreeeeek! Kreeeeek! behind me.

Eh, just shut up already! The rest of us would like to sleep now!

I yawn again and walk under the bed. I coil myself up. I imagine more adventures tomorrow. I yawn again, and that's the last I remember of that place and time.

05.............   *Another New Morning*

I wake up. I'm surrounded in soft light. As my vision clears it seems almost like I'm inside a vast white tent, stretching in all directions. I start to go back to sleep, but then I realize this is not a normal place to wake up. I open my eyes again.

Yes, I *am* under a tent. It looks like it's daytime outside. I see a heavy white sheet like canvas covering the entire tent floor, billowing with great waves into the distance.

Where am I? This is definitely not home. I'm too groggy-headed to be shocked.

I should say it's *like* a tent, but not squarely shaped. The ceiling looks mostly collapsed, touching the floor in areas. The ceiling billows even more than the floor, and there are no vertical walls or windows. There is no discernable exit.

I begin to faintly remember a strange dream of being a cat.

Yes, I was a cat yesterday. Was it yesterday? I'm regaining my senses.

I wasn't just a cat – I was Fluffy, Sharon's cat. Yes, I definitely was! That was no dream! What happened? How did it happen? Where am I now? What is happening to me? Today is different from yesterday, but it's still not *normal*. No, not at all.

»✳✳✳«

Boom! I hear a thundering noise from somewhere. Did a meteor fall out there? What was that? It's definitely not safe here, wherever I am.

I look up and see a bright glow through the thick fabric that might be the sun.

Boom! A similar noise goes off. I decide I have to get outside and see what's happening. I'm not about to stay in here.

I start to scurry along and reach one end of the tent. Yes, I said scurry. I'm shuffling along on all fours. This isn't normal.

Yes, it *is* normal, a voice in my head says. I have always gone on all fours. What other way is there?

Who said that? I *have* lost my mind.

I try to make sense of my situation. Am I still a cat? No, it doesn't quite feel the same, though I'm surely not myself. This sucks.

I look around, but I can't see any door or flap.

Boom! A noise thunders again. I begin to panic.

"There's no way out!" I squeak. Seriously, I squeaked.

I have no time to try to understand why this is. I turn and scurry to the other side. I can see no exit here either. I start to frantically push against the tent wall along the perimeter, and after a few seconds, whoosh! I slide down, and plop! I land.

It's a surprisingly soft landing, though I'm sure I must have fallen ten stories at least! I'm now standing on a rough, soft surface.

I think back to what it was like the previous morning. This surface is very similar, but even thicker and deeper. Yes, it could be carpet.

I look around. The light is unbearable! It's so bright it's eating away at my eyes. I must find shelter.

I turn and squint up to see a high ledge behind me completely open underneath, and I run under it.

Boom! Another thundering noise echoes.

Where am I now? How could I be under a tent one moment, and free-falling the next? And now I'm under some ponderous overhead structure. What are those noises? Is the bright light from the sun? It appears to be very close.

I look over to see a giant brown pillar seeming to support the vast structure overhead. I scurry over to it and find that it has a huge wood grain pattern.

What kind of giant tree was this made from?

Boom... Boom... Boom... Boom, I hear smaller eruptions in succession and growing louder. Whatever it is, I realize it's coming closer.

I turn toward the noise and scurry over to that side to see what's going on, terrified of what it might be.

Are the smaller noises related to the big ones?

Boom... Boom... Boom... Boom, the sound comes closer. Boom... Boom!!! Boom!!! Out of the foggy distance I begin to recognize...

Oh, no!

A mammoth creature beyond dimension ever so slowly strides closer. It's so big its upper extremities fade into mist. I can only generally make out two massive legs as large as a brontosaurus, but it has huge flat feet the size of cars!

I panic and find myself running in circles, even out into the searing brightness.

Aaauuurrr! The blundering monster roars, and Boom!!! Boom!!! Boom... Boom... The thundering rumbles away.

I only panic more at all this commotion, but manage to scurry back away from the light and under the shelter.

Boom... Boom... Boom... Boom, the thundering footsteps of the colossus fade away. My heart is pounding, and I shuffle back over to the massive wooden pillar I had examined before, for some modicum of security.

What was that monster? There is no creature on Earth that large. I remind myself that I'm not myself, and just yesterday I was turned into Fluffy the cat. Anything seems possible now.

Even though I had become a cat, I was in my own house. This place seems similar, yet very different. It's entirely too large a space to be indoors. Still, the floor seems like it could be carpet. Have I become even smaller?

I'm still in a panic, and I begin to realize there is some way I'm supposed to go – some place to escape. I can't remember!

Thoom... Thoom... Thoom... Thoom... A more insidious noise starts coming closer.

Uh-oh, I've heard that before. Something is telling me to get out of here! Yes, there is some way out of here. Where is it?

I start to run in circles again. Thoom... Thoom... Thoom... Thoom... The noise comes closer.

I turn in the same direction I saw the colossus before. Into view rumbles a smaller beast, but still many times the size of me. Thoom! Thoom! Thoom! It's the size of an elephant – and it's coming straight at me!

The beast lowers its head under the shelter. It's a giant cat! It looks just like Sharon's cat, only a hundred times larger!

Somehow this is not unusual. No, not unusual at all, I hear a voice say. Those giant beasts are the great enemy. Yes, they always have been. What else could they be?

Rrrauwww! The giant cat roars and lunges toward me. I bolt to the side and scamper in a straight line, and thump! I crash into a wall.

I try to gather my wits as the giant cat bears down on me. I look back and it's only a couple of slow strides away. I turn back toward the wall.

I've seen this before. Yes, it's coming back to me in the nick of time. Turn left and in a few strides is the escape!

I jump in that direction and the cat scrapes its terrible claw against the wall right where I had been.

Yes, there it is!

I squeeze through a hole in the wall and into the dark.

An Unusual Realization

I stand in a confused daze just inside the hole I dove through. It's utterly dark and I can't see a thing. I hear the horrid cat on the other side as it scrapes its claws at the hole, and, ow!

It's grazing against... my... tail...? I have a tail? Ow!

Yes, of course I have a tail, I heard in my head. I always have. What else would be back there?

Ow! The cat's claw is pinching the tip of my tail!

I lurch inward to pull free and turn to see the massive claw reaching through the hole. The intense light from the other side flashes on and off as the giant paw passes back and forth.

I turn and squint to see my surroundings illuminated by the strobing light as my chest heaves from the constant fright that the morning has been.

At least I think it's morning. It was certainly bright out there. Actually, the sun was straight overhead. No, that wasn't the sun.

I squint to see that I'm now in an alley, completely dark aside from the light through the hole. I notice great clutter on the floor. There are massive wads of a hairy-looking white material.

The strobing stops – apparently the cat has given up and moved on to other horrors. I can't stand the intense light pouring through the hole another instant.

I turn and slowly make my way down the alley. As I go I begin to recover from so long in the glaring light. I can see better where I am now. I navigate the clutter, having to climb over it at times.

Yes, now the light is much better. I try to gather my thoughts. What am I now? I'm not a cat. I'm much smaller. I scurry along on all fours. I squeaked when I tried to talk. I have a tail.

And *where* am I? I begin to connect the dots. It couldn't be a coincidence that I saw a giant cat that was the same colors as Fluffy. It must have been Fluffy. If that was Fluffy, the giant monster must have been Sharon!

So, I'm still in my house? Where am I now? Where was it that I woke up? I fell very far down out of the tent, and then I was under that giant overhanging structure that the tent seemed to be on top of. I didn't get much of a chance to look at it, with Sharon and Fluffy terrorizing me.

Hmm, wait. The dark wooden pillar… I think that was my bed! I woke up on my bed under the sheets, and I fell out of the bed on the floor! The great light above was the ceiling light of the bedroom. Why did it seem so bright?

Yes, I shrank again! I shuffle on all fours, I have a tail, I'm much smaller than a cat, I squeak when I talk, and a cat chases me? I'm a mouse! Yes, Sharon came into the bedroom, saw a mouse, and sicked Fluffy on it. And *it* was *me*!

I ran through a hole into the wall. It's the same hole I chased a mouse into yesterday! Did I chase myself into this hole? This is getting deep. What is happening to me? And why? What have I done to deserve this? I want my life back!

I try to gather my wits yet again. I don't want to be a mouse, but I have to survive. I definitely don't need to be going back into the bedroom. One encounter with Fluffy is enough.

I continue on inside the wall away from the hole.

So, this is what the inside of the wall looks like. It's a mess in here!

I continue to plod along, and I reach a turn to the left.

This is quite familiar. Yes, a regular haunt. I've been here many times. Yes, there is the turn back to the right. And just a bit further, there is another right and the beginning of the great slope upward. Yes, I have been here before.

I reach the slope and hustle up it, on and on. Upward and upward I go. At the end of the ramp is an opening. I creep warily up to it.

There is a faint light, but this is obviously not an open space, so I guess there must be no great danger. I step up through the opening, and realize it's an intersection. Cluttered alleys go left, right, and straight ahead.

Now which direction do I go? My memory is a bit fuzzy. I look to the right – that alley extends into the distance. Yes, that seems familiar.

I look back to straight ahead – another hall extends into the distance. There seems to be a hole some way down it where light pours in.

I look to the left, and Aaah! What is that?

I shuffle back down the ramp in a panic. It was a giant rat staring me in the face! I burrow brainlessly into one of the piles of fuzzy stuff. I keep kicking my legs trying to dig further in and hide.

Wait, I hear something. Is someone talking to me?

"Oy, Tib! What are you doing?" I hear a voice say.

Huh? Who was that? Is that giant rat talking to me? It can't be. I keep trying to dig to safety.

The voice comes closer. "Hey, quit screwing around!" The sound is definitely right behind me.

Ah, I realize now. I know that voice. Of course I do. It's my buddy Nib. Yes, I know him.

I back out of the hole I'd dug. I was probably only half-way in anyway.

"What is with you Tib?" I hear the voice say, but it would not properly be called a voice. There were sounds, squeaking sounds.

Yes, this is the way of talking. This is how we communicate. How else would you?

I turn around to face him. Oh, right. It's only a mouse, and the same size as me. This is a big spotted black mouse. My buddy Nib. We've been pals forever.

"Well? What's gotten into you, Tib?" he squeaks.

"S-Sorry, Nib. I-I'm just n-not myself t-today," I haltingly squeak in reply, the art of mouse-speak coming back to me.

Nib shakes his head in annoyance and turns around, heading back up the ramp.

Yes, yes of course. I'm a mouse. My name is Tib. Always has been. What else would I be?

I notice my nose right before my eyes. Yes, it is quite a protruding, hairy nose. I look down at my hands. No, no hands there. There are two brown-colored claws stretching out under me. Yes, I am a brown mouse. That is me.

"Oy, Tib! Get a move on!" I hear from the opening above.

I come to my senses and scurry up to follow Nib, who disappears from sight. I reach the top, but I can't see him,

Where did he go? I turn right and scurry into the passage.

"This way!" Nib hisses at me from behind. "Don't go that way! What is wrong with you?" he squeaks like a whisper. "You go that way and you'll find yourself in Rit's nest! Are you crazy?"

I turn around and shuffle up to Nib. Yes, left was the correct direction. I remember now. You don't mess with Rit. He's a dominant male, and doesn't kindly welcome male guests to his nest. No, not at all.

I step into the intersection and notice air movement. I can feel it with my whiskers. I cross into the passage where Nib led. I can also feel the walls with my whiskers. I follow Nib down the hall, and shortly it turns to the left.

"I'm hungry," says Nib.

Ah, yes. Food. "Me too," I reply.

I follow him down the passage. Next we reach the jumping section. This consists of narrow landing areas separated by wide openings.

You have to be a good jumper here. There's a straight fall all the way down to the next level with no place to grab onto if you miss a step. I have no fear of this at all. I'm an excellent jumper with good grip. I follow a jump or two behind Nib. He's a talented jumper too, but his best skill is straightaway speed. I'm not afraid for him. We've done this many times. It's a good dozen leaps before we're across. The passage continues for quite a while more.

I'm starving more than ever. Boom! I hear a muffled noise. This is quite normal. The humans are always making great noises during the day.

We finally make it to the end of the passage and take a right turn.

Ah yes, the climbing section. I love to climb too. These walls have places to get a good toe-hold. I'm really good at this. We scale on down a long, long way. I follow behind Nib, who must also be famished, because he's heading down faster than I've ever seen him go before.

Yeah! I bound down behind him, gracefully shifting (or so it seems) from toe-hold to toe-hold, with all fours. It takes no time to find the bottom. I see Nib heading to the left and I follow him.

Ah yes, food is just around the corner.

I follow Nib through the hole into the eating space. Thankfully the door is closed, and there is no blinding light. My poor eyes can't take any more light today.

We scurry over to the food source. It's an endless supply of wonderful pieces of food. They're white and crunchy, and every one looks and tastes the same as the last one. Nib munches away on one, standing on his hind legs and balancing himself with his tail.

There's a hole at the base of the giant bag that contains the food to mine the treasure inside.

Craumph, I take a big bite. Munch, munch, munch. There's enough to feed us forever. Craumph, munch, munch, munch. Yes, that hits the spot. But there's not much moisture in it. I need something to drink.

Just then Nib shuffles away. I drop a half-eaten piece and follow him. Blinding light streams through a wide gap under the door, and Nib is squeezing through it!

Oh, no. Drink is out there. My poor eyes!

I briefly peek out squinting to make sure the humans or cat aren't waiting, and then I close my eyes and use my whiskers to find my way under the drinking place across the way.

I scurry across the floor, and whack! I hit my head on the overhang. I find my way under and can finally open my eyes. Nib is lapping from a pool. Plop! Another massive drip falls into the pool and splashes at my paws. Drops of drink fall from the mysterious structure above us. I move up to the pool and drink my share.

A Day in the Life, Part 2

Nib and I are frequently naughty mice. While the rest are sleeping, we have adventures on some days. We've had quite harrowing experiences in the past. Yes, mice are supposed to sleep through the day – but not me and Nib.

Ahh, the drink is refreshing. Nib is already heading back. I follow. I squint this time instead of completely closing my eyes so that I won't whack my head again.

I follow Nib back under the gap and across the way to the pantry. Then, boom… Boom… Boom… Boom! I hear a human coming! I scurry in a frenzy and force my way through the gap.

Whew! I don't need any run-ins with those beasts today. I follow Nib as he heads back to the food source for another bite. I could use some more myself, I grab another piece and stand to munch it. Munch, munch, munch. Yes, this is the life!

We both finish about the same time and Nib nods to me. I follow him back through the hole and around the corner to the climbing area.

Yeah! I'm really feeling energetic now, and I bound up past Nib to the top.

He huffs and puffs as he catches up and says "Whew, that's the Tib I know!" We both pant for a bit, and then he says, "What do you want to do now?"

Boom! Another thundering noise comes from somewhere.

"This way," I call to Nib, and turn and sprint down the passage behind.

Nib races up with me. He knows where I'm heading. Nib has always been a fast runner. He has a longer tail than me, and better balance. He overtakes me at a turn to the right.

I pick up the speed and am on his tail. Nib isn't about to let me beat him. After a long sprint Nib has gained a little on me. He skids at a turn to the right, and thud! I crash into him.

"Hey!" he squeaks.

Oh yeah, we climb down here. "Sorry!" I reply, and while Nib pants in frustration I take advantage of the moment and leap past him, bounding from toe-hold to toe-hold down to the lowest level. Nib chuckles and follows after.

I reach the bottom and can hear Nib's panting behind me as we both try to catch our breath. My legs feel rubbery as I start to move down the alley and struggle to navigate the rubbish. We continue like this for quite a while until we finally reach the destination – a hole to the left into a large and dark space.

We never see the cat there at all, and the humans not very often. Plus, the light level is much more reasonable.

I pass through the hole, take an immediate left, and sprint on the smooth floor beside the wall. This side of this space has many large obstacles in it, with interesting passages to hide in between them.

At the moment I'm in the mood to stretch out my legs and run. Nib quickly sprints up from behind me and is gaining again. A giggle slips out of my mouth as I try to hold the lead.

As we run, I can see the strange lights along the ground coming up in the distance. I've always thought these curious. They run in two extended strips at the floor along the length of the wall ahead of us. The walls above those lights have a strange shape, with a large lip at the bottom. The floor in here always feels cooler than other ones inside.

I see Nib catching me on my left and just about to pass, and zip! I cut to the right well back from the strange lights. Ha! Nib goes sliding trying to make the turn. I always get a better grip than him.

I look back to see him regain his feet and start sprinting eagerly toward me. He yells something at me, but I can't make it out. I giggle again as I focus on running.

I know we were just past the obstacles on this side of the space before I turned. We are now running between them and the strip of light. I have to beat him this time. We're both sprinting in line with the long lights.

I'm just reaching the dark gap between the lights and the end of the obstacles on the right when bam! Ba-boom!!! Ba-boom!!! Ba-boom!!! An unbelievably loud rumble fills the vast space, and the second strip of light is growing vertically!

I skid to a stop in awe as the light grows upward, and I can begin to see the outdoors opening before me. The strip of light is a door – the biggest I've ever seen!

Crash! Nib slams into me and we both tumble into the growing, searing, outdoor mid-day light. It's a door to the outside! Ba-boom!!! Ba-boom!!! Ba-boom!!! The deafening rumble continues.

Nib and I regain our feet and stare at each other in shock.

What do we do? We both run around in circles, and thunk! we crash into each other again. We squint in the blinding light, and ka-pow! the rumbling comes to a stop.

Nib and I are just regaining our senses and are about to sprint back into the darkness when bumba… Bumba… Bumba… another rumbling sound is growing somewhere distant. We both sit frozen in petrified curiosity, and I realize the rumbling is coming from outside the door.

Bumba… Bumba… Bumba! The rumbling grows louder, and some massive beast, many times the size of a human, comes slowly thundering toward us. I can barely make out the vast shape in the intense glare.

We squeak and run in circles again, then we both manage to finally start running side-by-side in the same direction. I regain my senses and realize we are not running toward the darkness, but right through the heart of the lighted area!

It's too late now to turn back! We both keep sprinting, needing to find the far wall before we're trampled. A shadow passes over us, apparently cast by the approaching prodigious beast.

Yes! I can see the end of the light ahead.

Burrumba!!! Burrumba!!! Burrumba!!! The thundering grows and grows and the ground trembles. This is the most fearful beast I have ever encountered! Does it eat humans?

I kick in the speed and am actually passing Nib by. I'm just reaching the darkness, and then I hear a scream from Nib behind me.

Oh no! I try to turn around, but ssssch-thump! I slide and crash into the wall in the darkness.

I quickly get back on my feet and look toward Nib. My eyes adjust to the reduced light where I stand, and I can faintly see him squirming on the ground just across in the lighted area. Another black shadow passes over him.

"Look out!" I yell. I see him recognize in terror that the beast's back leg is coming down over him.

He scrambles out from under it just in time!

I rush over to him, and he squeals "Ow! Ow! Ow!"

He seems okay, but he points back behind him. I look back and the very tip of his tail is completely flattened!

"Wow, that was a close one!" I murmur.

"Easy for you to say!" Nib frantically responds.

The immeasurable beast that stepped on Nib's tail comes to a stop above us. We are in such awe that we continue to stand in the blazing sunlight.

"What is this thing?" I say, squinting.

We both look up at the expanse of the monster, fading into the distance as far as I can see. It is so large that its underside is hardly visible. It's a grey color underneath with a very irregular shape, like great muscles. Its sides are very shiny and smooth, of a grey-blue color.

As if this wasn't strange enough, it has the oddest paws and legs. I can't see the front leg very clearly from here, as the beast is so long that it fades into the mist, but I remember having seen it pass by, and it looked similar to the rear leg just in front of me. The leg and paw wrap up so smoothly that I can't tell where one ends and the other begins.

Even stranger are the colors of the legs. The outside is a dull black with a strange texture similar to the pads of a claw, except the pad seems to cover the whole leg and paw in a circle. Inside of that circle is a shiny silver color with holes in it.

I can see the sinews of the leg inside! This is the most bizarre beast. I can't see how it could move with legs like that.

Thunk! A huge noise comes from the beast, and we jump a step backward. A smooth rumbling sound comes from it, and it seems to be spreading out a vast wing.

We continue to stand dumbfounded, and then some great appendage begins to extend out toward us from behind the wing. We jump another step back.

Wait, this appendage is familiar. Yes, it's just like the leg of a human! It reaches all the way to the ground not a long distance from us. I then see another identical appendage beginning to stretch out.

"I've seen enough!" I yell. "We've got to get out of here! This way!"

I indicate to Nib to follow me, and we sprint into the darkness by the wall behind us and follow that wall away from the beast toward the corner where it meets the wall with the vast door.

We could escape that way, but my eyes can't take any more light. I turn to look back to the beast. A human stepped out from it! It had been *inside* of it!

Is the human escaping? What kind of beast is this?

We cower in the corner fearing to see what will happen next. The human thankfully begins to lumber away from us, and the great wing of the beast slowly retracts. We are not going outside, so we decide this is the time to make our way back to the hole we had entered through. We carefully move along the wall now in the direction away from the huge door.

Ka-thwop! A thundering noise comes from the great beast as its wing fully retracts. It seems this beast is very docile in spite of the horrid noises it makes, and the human controls it.

How one giant gets inside of another bigger one and controls it I have no idea.

I keep looking back to make sure a cat or rat doesn't come in through the vast opening. The human has moved out of sight to the other side of the beast.

Boom! A noise comes from that direction. I think it went through a door into another interior space. Doors make an awful noise.

Suddenly, bam! Ba-boom!!! Ba-boom!!! Ba-boom!!! The deafening rumble starts again. The violent noise makes it difficult to think, but I realize the great door to the outside is now closing. I stop and look back toward it.

"Come on!" Nib yells at me, but I ignore him.

It's closing from the top down, in reverse of how it opened upward. I've never seen a door open vertically. Then again, I've never seen a beast other than the humans open a door and lumber through.

I turn back and we continue to move away from the closing door. After a while we reach the corner where the wall we walked beside meets the far wall opposite of the great door.

Ba-boom!!! Ba-boom!!! Ba-boom!!! The unendurable rumbling continues, and then pow! it comes to a stop, and utter darkness falls. After a period of echo there is silence.

Nib and I look at each other as our eyes adjust back to the normal darkness.

"Whew!" I say, and we begin to chuckle from surviving the excitement.

Bang! Not silent.

"What was that?" Nib says.

"I think it came from the great beast," I reply.

More time passes and we wonder what will happen next. Still silent. We begin to make our way to the exit from this dangerous place.

Bang! Another noise from the beast. I can see quite well now, though the beast is so expansive that it fades into the misty distance above. I'm certain it has not moved one bit since the human exited it.

"That's strange," I say.

"Yeah," Nib answers. "It makes this loud noise from time to time, but doesn't budge."

"A strange beast," I respond. "The humans have trained an even larger beast to serve them for transport I guess. It certainly is docile."

"Yeah," Nib replies. "This reminds me of the legend of our distant relatives that carry their young in pouches on their stomachs. I've never heard of such a creature carrying humans."

"It's no relative of ours," I respond.

We both stare up at the amazing colossal beast. We then carefully find our way back to the hole in the far wall where we entered before.

We make it inside, and Nib says "some fun you found us! Now it's my turn."

I was in no position to argue. "How is your tail?" I ask.

"Numb, I guess," he answers.

I suppose the flattened bit will fall off some time later. "Sorry about that," I say.

"Not your fault. You outran me at the end there, and that was the difference."

Hmm, yeah, I did do that, didn't I.

"Try to catch me now!" Nib squeaks, and he bounds back down the passage, dodging deftly through the clutter.

I follow right behind him, and we reach the climbing section. He's fired up now, I can tell, as he bounds up all the way to the next level far before me.

I reach the top and he isn't there. I sit panting, and then I hear him squeak from even further above.

Ah, I know where he's going.

I climb up after him. I reach the next level up, and Nib is waiting. He's already calmed down by now, but my chest is heaving.

"Ha! I've still got it, even with a bum tail," he says.

I nod as I huff and puff. He then turns and heads toward the hole into another space, the highest one. Down one passage, a left turn, down the other for a while, and then the hole is on the right side.

The best thing about this space is there is almost never a blinding light or a human. The cat is never up here, but there are rats sometimes. A mouse must absolutely avoid rats.

I'm still panting as I follow Nib through the hole. Boom! Another huge noise echoes from somewhere.

The second best thing about this area is there are many opportunities for jumping and climbing, my two favorite pastimes.

Whooash! A loud noise comes from nearby.

"What was that?" Nib says.

I step up beside him. I can hear a low roaring sound from the same direction. We move cautiously toward it. I've seen this before, but I haven't heard it make such a noise like it did before the roaring.

The noise comes from an immense white tower stretching upward out of sight. A pulsating blue light comes out of a hole a good distance up from us.

The rumbling noise sounds normal, so we decide there isn't a threat.

"I've built up quite a thirst with all this running about," says Nib, and he walks right up to the tower.

Ah, yes. Drink can sometimes be found under there.

I walk up beside him, and he's already buried his head under the rim. I step up and stick my head in, and yes! there is something to drink on the floor under the tower. There's a gap under this tower similar to the drink source we visited earlier, except that one is not a rounded tower. It's black and square.

The inside of this one is very different, and I've never seen where the liquid comes from. The space underneath is too tight to explore. Plus it's a little stuffy under here and the rumbling sound is a little disconcerting.

I just want to get some drink and move on. I lap up quite a bit. Ahh, that's refreshing. I pull my head back out. Nib is waiting with a smirk on his face. He tears away sprinting into the distance. I grin and sprint right behind him.

We run over a long expanse of the floor, and I'm able to catch up to Nib just before we reach the climbing wall. Half of this great space is at a lower level (the one we entered at), and the other side of it, beyond the climbing wall, has a considerably higher floor. Actually, it's not a floor like the lower side. I sprint past Nib and leap onto the climbing wall, bounding up it quite athletically (or so it feels). I stand at the brim and then Nib heaves himself up next to me.

The higher side is the most fun of all. Instead of solid ground, there's an array of narrow ledges separating the whole expanse into sections. After a good drop, the bottom is filled with a soft, white pillowy material.

In fact this material is similar to the stuff that clutters inside the walls, but there's an endless supply of it up here. We make our nests out of the stuff.

The expanse of it in this area is great fun to land on, but it's not easy to get out of. Nib fell in one time, and I fell in after him, and we barely were able to make it back up to the ledge.

The fear of another spill doesn't daunt Nib, as he springs out onto the next ledge over, and jumps from there to the next after that.

I'm not about to let him beat me at my specialty, and I leap from ledge to ledge, passing Nib before we reach the last one, which is right next to the far wall. We both huff and puff to catch our breath and laugh for the fun of it.

Nib starts walking down the ledge toward the other side. I decide I'm in the mood for something more challenging, so I leap back to the previous ledge and stick the landing.

Yeah, no problem. I easily balance myself and walk gracefully (or so it seems) down the ledge parallel to Nib. My plan develops a flaw as I reach a great pillar stretching upward out of sight. It mounts directly on top of the ledge, blocking my path.

"Whatcha gonna do now?" I hear Nib wryly ask from the other ledge.

I look back from him to the situation to figure out just what I *am* going to do. Hey, no problem. Nib can't see, but there's another ledge just below the top which runs perpendicular to the ledge on the opposite side of mine from Nib's, in line with the pillar.

I jump down onto the lower ledge and then back up on the other side of the pillar. As far as Nib could see, I disappeared behind the pillar and magically bounced back up on the other side. After executing the maneuver, I stand on my hind legs, balancing myself with my tail, and casually place a forepaw on the pillar to my left, confidently facing Nib.

"How the heck?" he questions, and I just humbly shrug my shoulders.

Ha! I dart down the ledge toward the far wall, where a section of level floor extends away from the array of ledges. I take a sharp right turn when I reach it, and run back toward the climbing wall to the lower part.

Nib catches up, and I look back to him. He still has a puzzled look on his face at how I managed that move. I look down to the lower level.

Hey, is that dinner? I can see a large chunk of enticing looking stuff mounted in some kind of device. I look over to Nib, and he has a worried look on his face.

"Be careful," he says.

I trust him, and I climb down and walk over toward the contraption, but not too close. Nib steps up next to me to analyze it.

"I've seen one of these before," he says.

I look at it myself and there is definitely something familiar and foreboding about it. It's a large platform, with some configuration of bars on it.

I sniff, and can smell the chunk that's mounted in there. It's definitely food. It smells delicious, and I take a step forward.

Nib stops me, placing a paw on top of one of mine. "Don't take another step," he says. "You remember old Nit?"

"Um, yeah."

"Rit told me once he saw Nit come upon one of these things. He said he saw from a distance Nit step onto the thing, and then thwop! the bar snapped over and crushed him!"

I look in horror at Nib as he soberly stares at the device. "Rit said he couldn't get him out of the thing, and old Nit wouldn't respond. He said he had to leave him there, and when he brought helpers back, the whole thing, including Nit, was gone. Nobody every saw him again."

"Whoa." The story is very frightening, yet I'm still curious about getting at the food inside the device.

I look back over at the contraption and get an idea. I don't know where it came from, but I feel I have some idea about how this thing works.

I look around and I see a long blue object. I walk over to it, nudge it with my nose and it rolls over. It's a big tube with a protruding seam along one side and slanted ends. It's about as long as Nib's tail, flattened part and all, and twice the diameter.

I reach out my paws and try to pick the thing up with them. I can't manage it. I reach down and bite the thing in my mouth, and try to lift it. No, too heavy. I can just get one end off the ground, but I can't carry it.

I finally pick it up on one end in my mouth and drag it over to the contraption. Nib has watched me the whole time in a state of confusion and concern.

I somehow know that I can trigger the device with the big tube. I drag the tube over and line it up perpendicular to the long side of the platform. I pick it up at the end furthest from the platform, but I'm not strong enough to lift the other end off the ground at the same time.

It comes into my mind to bite it with a short amount hanging out of the side of my mouth opposite the device. I don't lift it up so high this time, and I put my right paw over the end next to my mouth.

This time when I lift it up my right paw leverages it, and the other end lifts up. I try to move sideways to get the other end onto the platform, but I can't quite coordinate it, and the tube falls short. It slightly bumps the side of the platform, and Nib jumps back. He continues to stare at me warily.

I try the same method again, and yes! I get the other end on there this time.

Okay, now I think if I push this tube against the block of food I'd like to get my paws on, it should trigger whatever happens that you don't want to be caught under, or maybe I can knock the food off the other side.

I drop the end of the tube and reposition myself to push it into the block. I lift it up in my mouth and push. Umph! Nothing happens.

"What are you doing?" I hear Nib ask.

I pull back and push it again. Umph! Nope. I look back to Nib, who stares at me with his head cocked sideways in an exasperated expression.

I draw back as far as I can without the tube falling off the platform, gather all my strength and heave! I slam the tube into it. Ouch! the sharp end digs into the roof of my mouth!

The pain from that somewhat distracts me as I see a big loop of a bar on the contraption swing across from Nib's side to the other, and wham! it slams ponderously down.

The tube (still in my mouth) is crushed by the bar, and the force makes it pop up out of my mouth and bash me on the nose. Ow! I don't see it as it happens, but the block of food is propelled in the air toward Nib, and he reflexively stands up and the block slams into his chest and he falls over still grasping it in his front paws, flat on his back.

Ow! My nose is throbbing, and the roof of my mouth hurts. I rub my nose on a paw. I look over to see Nib on his back, still grasping the prize.

I walk over to Nib, and he rolls over and stands up on his hind legs, still holding the block, with a shocked look on his face. I start laughing at him. He starts laughing at me as I rub my sore nose. He looks down at the block and sniffs it. His eyes bulge with excitement, and he takes a big bite.

"Hey," I yell, "give me some of that!"

I scurry over, grab it out of his paws, stand up on my own hind legs, and take a big bite.

Yum! That is good stuff. Yeah, that was worth it.

We split the rest of it, and we both look over at the contraption as we munch. The violence of the action has left the platform deformed. When we're done eating we walk over closer to it and cautiously inspect it. The bar loop dug into the platform and made a big crack in it.

Wow, there was definitely some malice behind that. Why, oh why, is a mouse's life so full of enemies?

"It's getting late," Nib says.

"Really?" I guess time does fly when you're having fun.

"Let's go have a look outside," Nib says.

We head back to the hole where we came in, but first we get another drink under the white tower.

A mouse doesn't normally drink so much, but we've been running, jumping, and climbing practically the whole day. Plus, we're *supposed* to be sleeping during the day.

After a quick drink I follow Nib back out of the hole. We take a right from there, and follow the passage to the outside wall on that side.

We take another right, and head down a long passage on the outer wall. That one is notorious for the clutter, and it takes a while to trudge through it.

We reach an opening on the right and go that direction instead of straight. The floor drops out quickly, and we climb all the way down to the next level.

We turn from there and head back to the outer wall and take a right at the tee there. We continue on down that passage until we reach a corner, and that directs us to the right. A bit down that way and we find a hole on the left side.

That one passes through the thick outer wall. It's a craggy passage, and it takes quite a squeeze to come outside. I follow Nib out.

Yes, it is quite dark out now. I squeeze all the way out, and drop down a short distance onto a sloped exterior surface.

That surface is large overlapping planks that have small rocks glued to them, so the whole thing is a rough array of rocks. It's a little tricky to walk across that and not get a sharp rock jammed up into your paw.

I look up as I gingerly walk across and I see a large brown mouse with Nib. Oh yeah, that's Rit. He's really a softie at heart, but you don't want to come near his nest when he's home, especially when he's sleeping.

I look back down to watch my step as I make my way to them.

"Hey, Rit," I say.

He scowls at me. "You boys been up all day again?"

Nib and I look at each other and smile sheepishly. Rit shakes his head in dismay. The fatigue of a day spent running around hits me at that point, and I yawn and stretch out.

I then carefully walk past them to look over the edge. It's a long way down there, but I can see that the bird bath far below is full to the brim.

I turn back to Nib and he's shaking his head. "Don't try it," he insists.

I've jumped off before and landed in the bath. There's nothing more exhilarating than that, plus swimming is my third favorite pastime. My stomach is fairly flat and I can use it to slow the fall somewhat. I even totally missed the bath once due to a wind, and landed softly on the grass with no injury.

I can't see what there could be to be afraid of.

"It's night-time," Rit warns. "You know there are beasts prowling about outside at dark."

Hey, if I can survive what I've seen so far today, I can do this. I lean over the edge.

"Don't!" cries Nib. "Come on Tib, I'm tired. We should get some rest."

He yawns and stretches, and seeing this makes me yawn again. Maybe I should go to bed. I look back down at the bath below. Boy, a swim would be great. What the heck. I forget the advice I'd gotten and leap out into the air.

As I fly majestically (as it seems) off the ledge, the cool evening air blowing through my fur as I fall, I hear Nib and Rit yell "Nooooo!" in fading voices above. I look down as I plummet straight to the center of the bath.

Splash! I land and go under, my paws just touching the base before I come back up. The water is disturbed with tremendous waves, and it takes some paddling before I can get a breath at the surface.

I swim over to the edge of the bath. Ahh, how refreshing. But I forgot what a shock it is to belly-flop from so long a drop, though. My stomach is a little sore.

I stabilize myself with my paws on the edge and look up to the ledge from where I had jumped off. I can barely see it up there, and I can't see Nib or Rit at all.

What's to worry about? I take a few laps around in the bath. Wow, this is great, I just love swimming. Ahh, this is just what I needed to relax after a busy day. I soak in the water, holding onto the edge with my paws. I almost fall asleep.

Okay, I better get going. Time to get some sleep in my nest. I pull myself up to the edge. I look over at the outside wall and remind myself where the way back in is. Yes, it's over in that outside passage a short way to the side.

I shuffle my hind legs until I get them up on the edge, and then leap off onto the grass. I land softly. It is quite a pleasant evening. There's no wind to knock me about. I shake my whole body to fling off the water.

Then, scraup! I hear a strangely familiar, foreboding sound behind me. I hear something moving through the grass. I turn cautiously around to see. I can't see anything. I stand up on my hind legs to get a better view.

Oh no! It's a massive brown rat! The most fearful creature to a mouse! I'm done-for this time!

I drop quickly back down and try to hide in the grass. This is no good, the rat saw me. I rack my brain to think of what to do. I decide the best thing is to make as fast as I can for the gap that leads to the way back inside, and hope to outrun the rat. I don't think the rat can fit in there, but I'm not sure.

I look in that direction and can see it's quite far away. But, what is that? Rit and Nib are standing in the passage! Nib is standing on his hind legs and motioning his front paws for me to get over there.

Just as I gather myself to spring and sprint for the passage, cra-a-a-a-ack! There's a loud, groaning sound off in the distance on the opposite side of me from the rat. I can see bright light shine out onto the grass.

I stand frozen. Little to my knowledge, the rat reacts the same way behind me, fortunately keeping some distance when he could have come up on me while I stood dumbfounded.

Shortly I see the light fade away, and stepping out is the second worse thing I could have imagined – a cat! I'm surrounded by the two greatest enemies of mice!

The cat slowly steps onto the grass, and then it notices something. It stops, looks straight at me, and its tail stands up. It crouches like it's ready to pounce, but it doesn't make a sound.

I turn to look behind me, and the rat is standing up with a stupid look on its face. It notices me, and suddenly remembers it wanted to get a piece of me – a big piece of me.

It bounds forward and starts toward me, stupidly forgetting that the cat could maul him too. I freeze again and crouch down in the grass. I turn to see the cat bearing down on me from the other side.

What can I do? I close my eyes and await my doom. Shortly I hear the rumbling footfalls approach from both sides, then a roar from both the cat and the rat, and then – a tremendous collision! The cat and rat roll in a great ball of fur away from me.

That rat is a goner. I can faintly hear Nib and Rit calling for me amid the roaring. I snap out of my stupor and sprint over to them. We don't look back and scurry down the gap to the hole back inside.

Once we're back in the wall, Rit says "you are a foolish mouse, Tib."

Nib shakes his head at me again. I stare at him still in shock, and then he smiles. Shortly I smile too, and we start laughing.

"What a day!" I say. "I am so exhausted!"

We reach the climbing spot and I barely have the energy to make it up. We're now close to the junction which leads in one way to Rit's nest, and the other to the exit to the outside ledge.

We say goodbye to Rit and head in the opposite direction to where Nib and I nest. We're bachelors, so there are no ladies in our nest. When we aren't bachelors, we'll have to settle down, lead separate lives, and sleep through the day. Someday that will happen, but not too soon I hope.

We reach our nesting area, and Nib burrows in across from me.

"Good night," I say.

I hear a muffled response from Nib. Good old Nib. We have good times together.

Before I even burrow myself in, I hear snoring from Nib. Yep, it has been a long and busy day. I dig into a nice soft pile of the fuzzy white stuff. Ah, yes, it's very warm and soft. The life of a mouse is good, even with all the enemies.

Ooooooahh, I let out a good yawn, and that is the last I remember of that place and time.

I wake up. It's dark.

Ugh, why am I awake? I haven't slept at all. Still, I feel somehow like it's time to get up. No, I've got to go back to sleep.

I start to dig into my nest to rest my head against a soft pillow, but then I realize I'm not in my nest at all. I'm lying on my stomach in the middle of an open space. I can sense walls nearby, but much further away than in the alley where we had nested.

How can I sense walls? I can't see a thing. How did I get out of my nest? What is wrong with my eyes? It's utterly dark.

What is going on? I don't know, but I'm starving. I have to get something to eat. I'm so hungry and driven to move that I just feel my way in spite of my lack of vision.

I wonder if I should wake Nib. No, this is crazy. Let him sleep. I walk a couple of steps.

Something is strange here. Where am I? Why can't I see?

I walk another step or two, and I run into a large obstacle. I try to walk around, but it's many strides wide and I can't find a way past it.

I wonder how I will get around the clump, and then boing! I jump forward right over the obstruction and a great deal past it!

Whoa! I love to jump, but I've never jumped that far! Or, have I?

Why yes, I've always jumped, I hear in my head. My rear legs are made for jumping. This is perfectly natural. How else would I get around? Walk everywhere?

Eh? What was that? I've gone delirious from lack of sleep! Or, maybe it's from lack of food.

I continue to walk. Yes, there is somewhere I should be going. This is the way to go. Turn right here and go down the wall. I will find food that way.

I begin walking down the wall. Uh! I'm walking *down* the wall? How am I doing this?

I've always walked down the walls, I say to myself. What else would I do? Fall to my death?

What? What did I say? What *is* going on? Something is wrong with my head. I have strange thoughts, I can't see, and I'm so disoriented I feel like I'm walking down the wall.

I continue on. It feels very much like walking vertically. I'm quite certain that I *am* walking down the wall. My, it's a weary long way. This is many times further than the distance between levels. Maybe I'm walking horizontally. I can feel that I'm near the end. Yes, here it is.

Hmm, I feel the wall ahead of me as if I have very long arms sticking out in front. Well, no, there aren't claws at the ends. They're like... Antennae. Yes, yes.

That *is* what they are, I think. I have two antennae on my head. Well, of course I do! How would I get by without them?

Did I say that? What has gotten into my head this evening? I don't have antennae – I'm a mouse! I definitely found a wall in front of me and am now walking across it. If I wasn't walking vertically before, I am now!

No, I was walking vertically before and now it's horizontal. I can feel it. I have to move on to get something to eat. Once I get some food in me and go back to sleep, my brain will work again tomorrow.

I continue on down the passage at this level. Boing! Boing! Boing! Three swift jumps in the dark.

Whoa! Did I do that?

Yes, I hear myself think, I do love to jump. It's so much faster than walking.

Huh? I love to jump, but I've never jumped like that! Ugh, I've got to eat right away!

I walk a bit more and find an opening that will lead to food. I walk through a hole into a great open space.

Wait, I've never been this way before. Where am I?

Of course you've been here before. This is the way to the food source.

What? What am I thinking? I still can't see well at all. This is definitely not normal!

>»*****«

Then my head starts to spin. I sense the world around me expanding.

Ow! My brain hurts. Ow! What is happening?

I suddenly begin to remember. I wasn't always a mouse. Ouch!

Yes, I know who I am. I'm Rupert Michael! Let me out of this nightmare!

I remember being the cat. I still must not be myself. Certainly not! I don't think I'm hallucinating. I must not be a mouse anymore. Do I really have antennae? How did I jump so far? Why can't I see? Why is this happening to me?

I want my life back! I want my car! I want my job! I want my wife! This is miserable! I want to be happy!

I ponder about the state of my life. *Am* I happy? Sharon and I haven't been getting along very well the last few years. My job leaves me perpetually exhausted. I feel like I'll never advance to a higher position. The state of the world is very frustrating and frightening. I feel powerless. It's not my fault!

Why does gas cost so much? Why is the world so full of enemies? Why does everyone refuse to do anything about it?

Aaaah! I try to scream, but I can't. I'm so confused! I'm trapped in a bizarre world, and completely freaked out.

I stand there – or lay on my stomach – I can't tell which, for a long time. I can't see a thing.

I finally accept that I can't escape, and decide I have to make the best of my situation. I'm starving more than ever. I have to eat. Yes, the food source is close by. It's to the left and just a few hops away.

I can see something. Yes, my eyes are beginning to function. I can't see very clearly, though. It slowly becomes clearer. My vision is returning.

I can see clearly now. I'm standing on a smooth surface that appears shiny in the small amount of light there is. I can't see very far, though. I can definitely say there is nothing very close to me.

I turn around and can see the hole I exited from. It's a gap in the molding. Wait, that looks much closer than the distance it felt like I came from it. I'm not a mouse anymore, am I.

I feel my stomach screaming again for food. Yes, I'm close now to the feeding area. I turn to the right. It's this way.

Boing! Boing! Boing! I jump and jump and jump toward the food source. Yes, I am definitely a jumper. I didn't jump like this as a mouse, and I could see best at night. I am definitely something else now.

Wait, what is that? I see a train of creatures a fraction of the size of me marching across the floor. I step closer to them. It's too dark to make them out clearly.

What are these things? I don't clearly remember. Something tells me I should avoid them. They're small, maybe one fifth of my size, but I think they're dangerous in numbers, and there are definitely a lot of them. Actually there are two parallel trains of them, going in opposite directions. They don't seem to notice me, so I'll just try to avoid them.

Ah, I remember – the food source is near. Somehow I know this. It's a most magical place. I come back every evening, and every time more food is there – lovely huge morsels with a little mold. Yes, it's coming back to me.

Wait, moldy food?

Yes, of course moldy is best, but I like to try some fresh food from time to time.

Huh? What did I just say? I really need to eat.

Boing! I jump right over the lines of marching creatures. Boing! Boing! Boing! I jump quickly clear of them and toward the food source. Boing! Boing! Boing!

Ah, I've arrived. I'm absolutely famished! Wait, there is something else here – some creature about the same size as me. Is it stealing my food?

I sneak up to one of the four great pillars that rain down the food from above. Yes, the food is always found in this area. There are four great pillars and many very large yet smaller ones all around the four. The smaller ones actually change their positions from night to night, search me as to how. This place is altogether magical. I sneak up to a pillar near the other creature and peek around.

Oh no! What kind of monster is this?

What is this creature? It's, it's, it's… A giant cricket! It's the same size as me! I'm doomed! What do I do? I stand frozen as a stone.

Hold on… Ah, yes. I should be getting the hang of this by now. I'm a cricket! Why, yes. It makes sense. The leaping legs. The antennae. Hmm, let's see… Yes, I can wave my antennae around. They look like his. My, his legs look so long and powerful.

Well, yes, of course they are. They always have been, as have yours! What else could they be? You've known Krick your whole life.

Yes, that does sound like a familiar name.

I step out from behind the pillar to partake of a morsel of the food. Krick notices me and turns around.

"Hey Scritch," he says.

I pause. Hmm, Scritch. Yes, that is my name. Wait, did he say that? I don't recall hearing words.

"Wake up, Scritch," I hear him speak again.

Am I imagining this?

"Hey Krick." Whoa, did I just talk? How did I do that?

"How's it goin'?" he asks.

"Pretty good, I guess. I'm a little drowsy-headed. I feel like I didn't sleep."

"Yeah, I wondered where you had headed off to. You're usually out here before me."

"I was up on the next level."

"Next level? What were you doin' up there?"

"I'm really not sure. But, ahh, this food really hits the spot. I'm beginning to feel like myself again."

I munch a big piece of food with a handsome growth of white mold on it. Of all the molds white is my favorite. Green isn't bad either. Sometimes I eat the food before it becomes moldy, but that is very wasteful. As great a gift as the food that falls from above is, the growth of the mold is an equally wonderful gift.

"Yeah, it is amazing isn't it?" Krick says with a full mouth, watching me eat, and he looks upward, continuing to speak as small bits of food fly out of his mouth. "How we've been blessed by heaven to receive such bounty is just amazing. Just amazing."

He continues to munch away, starting on another morsel. He finishes that one and then gobbles up all of the crumbs he had spewed at his feet.

"Ahh," he says after a moment and starts stretching out. "It's time for you to go, Scritch. I'm gonna call the ladies."

I'm still a little groggy in the head at this point, so I don't know to immediately react when he says this. A second later I would be fully awake.

He lifts one wing and sets it to the ridge of the other like a violin and starts playing. Kreeeeek! Kreeeeek! Kreeeeek! The sound is ear-splitting!

I can barely gather myself to turn and spring away. Kreeeeek! Kreeeeek! Kreeeeek! I can feel my whole body vibrate. I had just started on a lovely piece of green mold, but had to drop it.

Boing! I take a clumsy hop. Kreeeeek! Ow! My ears! Boing! I jump as far as I can go. Kreeeeek! Ugh, he'll never stop! Boing! I jump again.

Uh! I land very close to the lines of marching creatures. Some start to approach me. Kreeeeek! Boing! I jump over the creatures. Kreeeeek!

Boing! Boing! Boing! I finally jump far, far away until I can't hear his hideous calling.

Wow, I am very certain Kreek has never, ever, gotten a mate with that call. How could anyone stand it? Mine is truly musical, not his. Ugh, I can't stand to think about his!

And what is it with those marching creatures? Oh, right, I remember. They also feed in that area. It can be a real pain if they decide to feed under the pillars, but they seem to prefer other foods thankfully. They don't stand there and eat. They carry pieces of it with them. One line passes in and another passes out with the food. I've seen them take the food into tunnels outside. You don't want to mess with them. They will generally leave you alone, but if you get too close they'll gang up on you. I've seen them bring down and eat an entire cricket. I don't want to become a meal for them!

Hmm, what was I doing? Oh yes, I should be calling now too.

I decide to head off to a different place. Boing! Boing! Boing! I remember a good place to go. Boing! Boing! Boing! I jump and jump and jump. Boing! Boing! Boing! I jump until I'm tired of it.

Boing! Ah, yes, here is the spot. Get over against the wall and get started.

I place my wings together, and screeeeetch! Screeeeetch! Screeeeetch! I play my song for all to hear. Screeeeetch! Screeeeetch! Screeeeetch!

"Come, my ladies, for an evening of romance!" I call. Screeeeetch! Screeeeetch! Boom!!! Screeeeetch! Boom-boom!!!

Uh! What is that? Boom!!! That is no lady! Boom-boom!!! That can't be good. Boom!!! Better... Hide... Ugh! Light! Get outta here!

I scramble along the wall, looking for a hole to climb into. Boom-boom!!! I manage to find a dark alley next to the wall. What is that noise? Boom! I sit there for a long time, and then the light goes away and all becomes calm.

Okay, I'd better hurry up with the call before something bad happens.

I crawl out into the open next to the wall, where all can hear me, and Screeeeetch! Screeeeetch! Screeeeetch! Boom!!! Screeeeetch! Boom-boom!!! Boom!!!

Oh no! Boom-boom!!! Boom!!! The light comes on again. What do I do? Boom-boom!!! Ugh, something is looming over me... It's blotting out the light...

Uh! I jump, and crash! There's a massive collision right where I had just been standing! Uh, here it comes again! Boing! I jump. Crash! Another jolting collision, coming after me! Boing! Boing! Boing! I jump like mad to get away for a long while. Boing! Boing! Boing! I jump until the light and noises are gone.

Kreeeeek! Boing! Kreeeeek! Kreeeeek! Boing! Oh, no, I've headed in my panic back toward Krick's infernal bellowing! Kreeeeek! Kreeeeek! Kreeeeek! I recoil in a maelstrom of tearing noise. Kreeeeek! Uh! My ears! Boing! Kreeeeek! Boing! Boing! Kreeeeek!

Boing! Boing! Boing! I continue to jump madly to some other place until I can't hear him anymore. Boing! Boing! Boing! I then stand still awaiting some other calamity, but nothing happens.

Okay, I must get back to the calling. I move over to the closest wall to get some good reverb, and screeeeetch! Screeeeetch! Screeeeetch! I call for lovers. Screeeeetch! Screeeeetch! Screeeeetch!

"Come and get it while it's hot!" Screeeeetch! Screeeeetch! Screeeeetch!

I pause, and can hear a faint sound.

"Is that the sound of love I hear?" Screeeeetch! Bump.

"Yes, I hear something sweet!" Screeeeetch! Bump. Bump.

Here come the hotties. Bump. Bump. Bump. Hmm, well, I think it's just one, but I have to take them one at a time anyway. Bump. Bump. Bump. Yes, this will be convenient. Bump. Bump. Bump. This will keep them from being jealous of each other. Bump. Bump. Bump. I don't need them fighting over me. Bump. Bump. Bump. I mean, who could resist my charms?

Bump. Bump. Bump. I can see her. Bump. Bump. Bump. Hmm, she is a big one. Bump. Bump. Bump. Oh my, she is a little manly for my taste. Bump. Bump. Bump.

"Is that you, Scritch?" I hear him call. Oh, good grief. It's Krick.

"What are you doing here?" I ask.

Bump. Bump. He walks up the last few steps. "I'm gettin' no action tonight," he says.

"Yeah, it does seem kinda slow. Plus, I had a scary time away yonder." I nod in the direction I had gone before.

"I'm gonna head over thataway and see what happens," he says, nodding in another direction.

"Catch ya later," I call, and he turns to hop away.

"It's no wonder you're shut out with that hideous bellowing," I say under my breath.

Krick stops and turns back. "What?"

"Nothing."

"I heard you say something," he persists, as he walks back toward me.

"Wasn't me," I say, trying to look innocent.

"Oh, yeah?" he raises his voice. "Who else do ya see 'round here?"

"Really, I didn't say anything!"

"Mmm-hmm. You asked for it."

He sets his wings together and Kreeeeek! Kreeeeek! he starts playing louder than ever! Kreeeeek! Kreeeeek! Kreeeeek!

I can barely think, and boing! I jump right over him, and whack! I bounce off the wall, thudding to the ground even closer to him. Kreeeeek! I feel the sound waves course through my body.

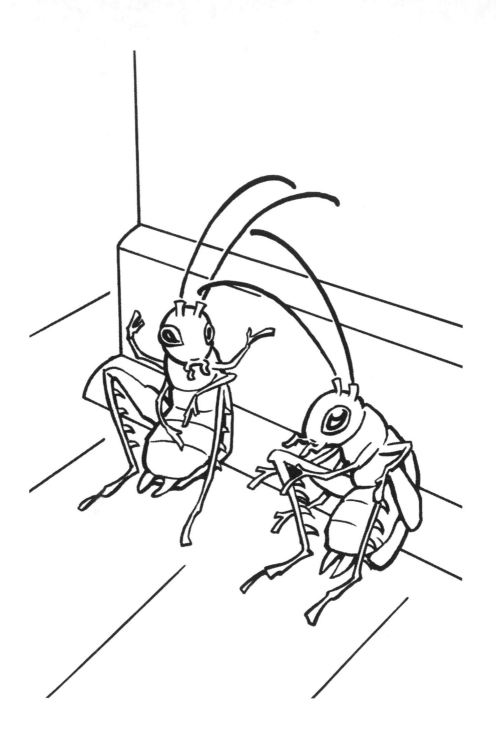

My ears won't last much longer. Boing! I desperately jump without thinking, trying to escape the stinging pain in my ears. Kreeeeek! Kreeeeek! Boing! I bounce off the wall again, but finally start jumping away from him. Boing! Kreeeeek! Boing! Boing! Kreeeeek! Boing! Boing! Boing!

Boing! Boing! Boing! I frantically jump and jump until I can't hear him anymore. Boing! Boing! Boing! Actually, I can't tell whether I'm out of earshot or if he has permanently blown out my ears. Boing! Boing! My head is ringing. Boing! I begin to walk, trying to shake it off.

Ooaah, I am sooooo tired! I feel like I didn't get good sleep last night. Hmm, and I'm still hungry too.

Doom, doom, doom-doom, doom-doom, at that moment I hear a growing noise.

Oh no, that can't be good.

Doom-doom, doom-doom, doom-doom! the noise grows ever closer, made by a creature much larger than me. Doom-doom! Doom-doom! Doom-doom! I see the great beast approaching. It towers over as it comes nearer, and I feel it swipe at me!

Boing! I instinctively jump as something passes below me. I land and the beast bears down on me again. It swipes at me, and boing! I jump right up into the side of the beast. It's very soft and hairy. I fall away from it back on the floor.

I hear the beast give a horrible low roar as it becomes even more determined to destroy me. I can sense the beast rearing back to jump at me.

Boing! I deftly jump backward, landing on my feet in the other direction, and boing! ka-pow! I leap away from the beast just in time to avoid being crushed. It's trying to pounce on me!

I don't wait to see what will happen next. Boing! Boing! Boing! I jump like I've never jumped before. Doom-doom! Doom-doom! Doom-doom! I can hear the beast pursuing behind. Boing! Boing! Boing! I jump as far and as fast as I can.

Doom-doom! Doom-doom, doom-doom, I hear the noise of the beast fade away. Boing! Boing! Boing! I jump until I can no longer hear it behind me. I take shelter under an overhang and hope to be free from further danger. I hope the monster hasn't gone after Krick.

I stand there for a long time, and finally decide to head back to the feeding area.

Krick should be able to take care of himself. He always has before. It must be safe now.

Boing! Boing! Boing! I jump. Imagine how long this would take by walking. Boing! Boing! Boing! Tsk, tsk, other creatures have to toil and walk. Boing! Boing! Boing! What a pain that would be! Boing! Boing! Boing! I've escaped from two gigantic beasts tonight as well as Krick's hideous noises.

Boing! Boing! Boing! I jump over the marching creatures again. Boing! Boing! Boing! I arrive at the feeding area. Krick isn't here. He's probably fine. I find a lovely half-molded crisp. Yeah, that is good stuff. I excessively stuff my face.

I'm very tired, but I feel my duty to call for the ladies one more time, so I give it another shot. I step into a corner, and screeeeetch! Screeeeetch! Screeeeetch!

I yawn. Screeeeetch! Screeeeetch! Screeeeetch! Ugh, I'm too tired. I have to sleep. This corner will do.

I tuck myself into the corner and fall fast asleep, and that is the last I remember of that time and place.

10............ Yet another Strange Turn

I wake up. Am I going to get any sleep? Even though it seems I slept only an instant, my brain is in a complete fog. Initially I can't say where I've just been or what I've done.

Maybe this is partly due to being in complete darkness. I initially get no feedback at all from my senses. I only know I'm awake and that I had very recently gone to sleep.

Slowly I remember that I've just been a cricket. I then realize I have my own consciousness. Rupert, that is. If I'm still Scritch the cricket, I'm no longer perceiving the world like he does.

I try to open my eyes. What? They're already open? I can't see a thing! I try to feel around. It feels strange, and I'm certain I'm standing on a hard surface. Yes, I am standing.

I was sleeping standing up? I've never sleepwalked before. Why is it so dark? Am I still a cricket? I try to gather my thoughts and determine where I am now. Yes, last night I went to sleep near the feeding area.

I begin to realize a pattern in my journey to this point. When I went to sleep Friday night I was in my bed. When I woke up the next morning, I was under the bed as the cat. When I went to sleep that evening I was back under the bed. When I woke up the morning after, I was on the bed again, but as the mouse. When I went to sleep that evening I was in the outside wall adjacent to the living room. I think I must have been on the second floor behind the fireplace and just on the bedroom side of the bay window to the back yard. I then woke up as the cricket in that general area.

It's a good thing I didn't try to wake Nib then, or he would have probably eaten me! I must have hopped within the wall above the window, come down the wall and out at the ground floor adjacent to the dining room. I took a left from there. Yes, I believe the feeding area of the crickets is under the dining room table! There is no doubt they could find fallen crumbs of food there. Or, that is, *I* could.

Am I still a cricket? Where am I now? There definitely has been a pattern of waking up as another creature near to where I went to sleep the previous night. The transition from the mouse to the cricket was different, though. It seems I woke up as a cricket not much later than I went to sleep as the mouse, if I slept at all. All of my recent activities were certainly during the evening.

Now it seems to still be evening. I can't see much. It doesn't seem like I slept at all this time, either. Wait, yes, I can see something. I can just vaguely see light. Either there is something terribly wrong with my eyes, or dawn is just breaking. I experienced something similar when I woke up as the cricket, but once I got out of the wall I began to see.

My vision isn't as good now as it was as a mouse, but I don't feel that it's unusual. Yes, I can now see that the light is increasing ever so slowly, but everything is very blurry. It seems almost like a myriad of double-visions. I shake my head, but there is no change. Yes, either something is wrong with my eyes or I'm not a cricket anymore. And I'm *definitely* not myself.

Given the previous pattern, I'm probably not a cricket now, and I must not be far from the dining room. I bet I'm in the dining room, possibly close to where I went to sleep before. Actually, if it is now dawn, as it seems it is, it must not have been long ago when I went to sleep.

I start to feel certain I'm not a cricket anymore. Do crickets eat whatever I am now? No, I don't think crickets go for live food. I hope not, anyway.

Wow, what a time I've had! If I get the chance I'll think better of Fluffy. Though, he does have a mind of his own. Being a mouse wasn't too bad. Nib was a good friend. Being a mouse was actually a lot of fun. I can't remember feeling so free. Even with so many threats, if you use common sense you can get by.

There's another obvious pattern. I've gotten progressively smaller. Human to cat, cat to mouse, mouse to cricket, cricket to… If I'm not a cricket I must be very small indeed.

I struggle to see where I am now. As the light gradually grows I can see more and more, but it's still blurry. Even though I can't see clearly, I'm now certain I have a bad case of double-vision. It would be better defined as multi-vision. I can see the same general shapes a number of times. Wait, they're not the same shapes. The shapes shift from image to image. It's like

I have an array of eyes that can all see at the same time. Unfortunately, it's all too blurry to make any details out.

I begin to realize a sensation that I'm supposed to go somewhere, and I feel less tired from lack of sleep. Yes, I can feel that I'm supposed to move just ahead. There is something that way that I'm supposed to do. What will it lead to? Can I trust my thoughts?

I take a couple of steps forward. Yes, this is different from being a cricket. My rear legs are the same size as my fore legs. Whoa, there's a large ditch in the floor just in front of me.

The light continues to grow. I'm certain it's now dawn. I begin to see movement. Yes, there are dark shapes moving before me. I feel an attraction to them. I think they are where I'm supposed to go. Am I supposed to fight with them? Am I supposed to join them?

Join them, I hear a voice in my head say. Join them. Take the path.

What? Join who? What path?

Hmm, yes, it begins to become clearer. I'm supposed to follow a path. The path will take me somewhere.

No! I'm not about to move until I can see clearly. As the light grows I can see the moving shapes are creatures about the same size as me.

I try to look around to see if I can locate a landmark to determine if I'm smaller than last night, but I can only see general shapes. I can't even make out details of the creatures right in front of me.

I can only tell they are creatures. They're walking on multiple legs. There are a lot of them. In fact, there's a never-ending stream. I can now see they're moving in both directions.

I still can't make out details. They seem to be fairly compact creatures. They're definitely not crickets. They're not jumping and the shape is different, not to mention crickets would not march like that. Yes, they are marching.

I definitely begin to feel I'm supposed to join them. Yes, they are following the path. I begin to feel comfortable. These are my comrades.

Yes, there is definitely a path I'm supposed to follow, just ahead.

The path will take me back to the colony, I think.

What? The colony? What is the colony? Hmm, I think it's coming back to me now. Yes, I have always been in the colony. The colony is home. It has always been that way. Where else would I belong?

I feel my brain changing again as it had before. Ugh, I feel sick. Whatever creature I am physically, I'm beginning to become it mentally as well. There is no use fighting it. Ow...

I'm not sure how I can sense it, but I can feel the path like smelling it, but different somehow.

Uh, wait a moment – I can sense strong vibrations. This is a threat. But, how do I sense it? Again, it's similar to hearing, but not the same. Somehow it seems my senses of smell and hearing are combined into something of its own. This is quite an interesting experience.

Yes. Well, no. It's not particularly special. This is the way it always has been. Of course, what other way could it be? I must get on the path. Yes, must get food!

I carefully step over the ditch in front of me and move into the train of moving shapes. Oh, pardon me. Get into line. Must follow the path!

I follow along on the path. We cross the floor. Yes, a very long way. Vertically up the wall. Over floors, up walls – there is no difference. Yes, this is perfectly natural. This is the path. Keep following the path.

It turns horizontally upside-down. Yes, that is where the path goes. Now it goes vertically again. Yes, yes, still on the path. Now horizontal on the top. Yes, I am on the top now. The food source is here.

Yes, yes, must pick up food. There it is. Rrrumph! Tear off a piece with my mandibles. Yes, take a piece of food back to the nest. Must serve the Queen!

Yes, I am an ant. Always have been. What else could I be? Yes, yes, take the food back to the nest. Follow the path.

Down vertically. Over horizontally upside-down. Down vertically. Keep following the path. Down, down, down. Follow the path. Over a big bump.

Now on the floor. Yes, we are on the floor. Careful with the great ditches. Don't lose your footing. Keep following the path.

Uh! I feel a vibration coming. Oh, no. Double-pace. Ugh, there is some collision behind. We are under attack!

11............ *A Day in the Life, Part 3*

We're under attack! Double-pace! Stay on the path! Must make it back to the nest! Must serve the Queen! Go! Go! Go! Turn left! The path turns left! Careful stepping across the ditch! Oh no, someone just fell behind me! Go! Go! Turn right! The path turns right! Stay on the path! Go! Just a bit further! Up a bit, darkness. Down a bit, light again.

Yes, we have made it outside. Stay on the path! Vertically down. Stay on the path. Horizontal. Stay on the path. Ugh, this section is very uneven. Swerve left, over a small bump, swerve right, over a small bump.

This continues for a long time. Thankfully I can't feel the vibrations anymore. Whatever it is is staying inside. I hope we haven't lost too many. Must serve the Queen. Must get the food to the nest. Ugh, still on this rough section. Stay on the path.

Okay, now going vertically down. Much smoother now. Stay on the path. Down to the ground. Yes, we are on the ground now. Stay on the path. I've always liked the ground. Very soft and comfortable, not like the hard floors inside.

The nest is not far now. Stay on the path. Weave between the grass stalks. Not far from home now.

Yes, I am an ant. I have six legs. I sense with my antennae. Yes, I have two antennae on my head. They droop down in front of my eyes. I have compound eyes. Not great for clarity, but excellent for coverage. If something moves I will see it – but my antennae are very sensitive and I most often sense a threat with them first. I can feel the grass stalks pass by. I can see their shapes pass too.

I can also sense the path. That's the way we ants find our way. The leader marks the path to the food and the rest follow, taking it back to the nest. Yes, must serve the Queen. Must follow the path. Almost there.

My mandibles are useful for many purposes. They are very strong. I can chop off a piece of food and carry it. I can hold up the weight of my entire body with them. Yes, here we are. We have reached the nest.

Down to the Queen! Ah, home sweet home. Must reach the Queen! Must drop off the food. Must serve the Queen! Turn left. Turn right. Go down. Turn right. Go down. Turn left. Go straight. Turn right. Go down. Turn left. Go down, very far down.

Yes, very close now. Turn right. Go down, Turn left. Go down. Turn left. Straight for a while. Go up. Turn left. Go straight.

Okay, here it is. Find a place for the food. That will do. Job done. On to the next task.

Now head back up to the surface. This time to the path on the other side. I understand there is a new food source there – a downed flying creature of some kind. Must gather food and return to the Queen.

Oh, and there are young workers in need of training. I must train one on this mission. Yes, this direction. You, follow me. Yes, you. Follow this way. I will train you. Move to the surface.

Yes, this is where the path begins. Keep following. Maintain the proper pace. Must train another. Yes, must keep the colony strong. All must do their part. Keep following. Maintain the proper pace. We're near to the surface now. Still behind? Very good.

Out of the nest now. Where is the path? There it is. Follow the path. Must follow the path. Still behind? Good. Must maintain the proper pace. Must gather food and return to the Queen. All must do their part.

Back on the ground now. Follow the path around the grass stalks. Still behind? Very good. Keep following the path. Haven't been this way for quite a while. We're not heading inside. This one is closer by.

Wait, I sense something. There is some commotion ahead. There is some danger. Stay on the path. Still behind? Maintain the proper pace. The disturbance is growing greater. There is some threat. Yes, there is certainly some threat. Stay back, trainee. Must maintain the proper pace. Stay on the path. Something is happening ahead. I can sense there is a battle. There is a threat. A great threat.

Still behind? Maintain the proper pace. Maintain control in a dangerous situation. Must serve the colony. All must do their part. Getting closer. Stay on the path. Maintain proper pace. Yes, we are getting very close. I can see movement. Some great beast is threatening the colony. Stay back, trainee. Must maintain discipline!

Must attack the beast! Must attack the beast! Double-pace! Stay on the path! Stay with me trainee! Must maintain proper pace! Go! Go! Danger! Attack! New path! Follow the new path! Climb! Climb! Follow, trainee! Climb! Climb! Clamp on! Clamp on! Bite! Bite! Hang on! Hang on! Bite! Bite! Hang on! This is a large beast! Bite! Bite! Hang on!

Ugh! The beast has cast me off! I have his flesh in my mandibles! Where is the trainee? Where is the trainee? I can hear you. I am coming. There you are. Well done! Follow me. Carry the flesh to the Queen! Back to the path!

Back to the path! There it is. Follow the path. Maintain proper pace. Return the food to the Queen. The beast has moved on. The danger has passed. Keep up! Must serve the Queen. Each must do their part. Follow the path. Not far from home. Follow the path. Weave around the grass stalks.

Almost home. Maintain proper pace. Return the food to the nest. Follow the path. Not much further now. Follow the path. Return the food to the nest. Keep following, maintain proper pace. Here we are. Home is near. Follow the path. Descend into the nest. Still following? Very good. Descend to the Queen. Deliver the food. Well done!

12............. The View from Below

Yes, now to deliver the food. Must serve the Queen! Still following? Good. You are familiar with this path. Very good. On, on to the Queen! Go down. Turn left. Go down, very far down. Turn right. Go down, Turn left...

Ugh, what is that? Ow, strange thoughts in my head... Ow! Something is wrong with me... Hold, trainee, maintain my pace. I must slow... Go down. Ugh. Turn left. What is happening? Straight for a while. Must deliver the food...

Go up. Ow, my head! Turn left. Ugh, I am defective... Go straight. I am a weakness – I have brought a threat into the colony... Yes, here we are. Drop off the food. Very good, trainee. Off with you. You are ready to forage on your own. Go! Must serve the Queen! Ow! What is wrong with my head? Ugh...

»»*»*«

Uh! Where am I? What is going on? It's so dark... Hey, don't push! What is that? People are rushing past me. Wait, are they people? I can't see clearly... What is this incessant movement? The ground is shaking. It's so violent I can't hear. I can feel every vibration.

Ow, my head hurts. What is this horrible place? How did I get here? I can't see. No, wait. My eyes are adjusting. I can vaguely make out moving shapes.

Uh! I am completely surrounded! Where am I? Hold on, I'm beginning to gain focus. I must have been knocked on the head somehow. I'm seeing the same image in a large array. Ugh, this is making me feel sick...

I try to focus on one of the array of images. What is marching past me?

Aaaaaah! They're giant crawling monsters! I'll be eaten! Please, don't hurt me! I've got to hide somewhere! Ow, my head! My brain is swimming… Why are they passing me by? Ow! Oh, my eyes… I can't… Focus…

What… What is this? I can see in all directions… My vision is becoming clear. It's as if I have eyes all over my head and can use them all concurrently! What is happening?

Argh! What are these creatures? They're… They're… Ants. Yes, man-sized ants filing madly past me! Disgusting! They don't seem to notice me. They bump into me, but go around without attacking.

Where am I? I see passages in all directions. Ugh… These creatures… So… Ugly. I've seen ants before, but from this perspective is quite another thing entirely! Yes, the shape of the body is familiar. Uh, but oh so large. Yuck! Don't touch me!

The legs move in a magical harmony of locomotion. Yes, they are quite efficient and powerful. The eyes are so large. They seem… Divided. Yes, each eye seems filled with an array of smaller eyes. Or, more like windows into blackness. They don't move.

Ugh, and the antennae… Two stalks stick out from the head and multi-segmented appendages hang down. They move about as if they're feeling around – like arms and hands. Ew!

Hey, what is hanging in front of my face? They follow my head. They're… They're… Antennae? No, no. I'm not in my right mind. Clearly not! Ow! Hey, no need to bump so roughly! Move around me like the others do!

Uh, what is this? The stick is moving as I think to move it… Yes, it moves as if it were my hand… Where is my hand? I can't seem to be able to lift it. Only this stick moves… No, it is no stick. It has multiple joints like the antennae of these creatures. Yes, I can move it. I can *feel* with it. Yes, I can definitely feel this wall.

Oops! The wall is not altogether stable. Pieces of it knock off. Uh, where, oh where, am I?

I feel trapped. I begin to panic. It's terrible! I try to look down and gather my nerve, but I can't stop seeing most everything around me.

How did I get here? Wait – what is that just ahead? Lots of white objects… I think I might as well move a bit forward, but I can't. I'm too afraid to move. I would close my eyes and wish for escape, but my eyes won't close.

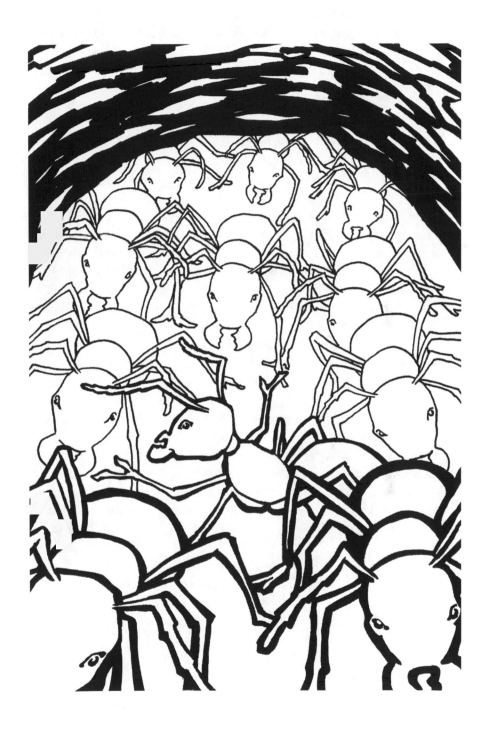

Ow! Ugh, some large stick is poking into my side. Ow! Hey! Quit pushing! I must move this stick. Ungh, here it is. Wait... Why did I pick this stick up in my mouth? And how can I hold it vertically?

The creatures that file by are holding things in their mouths – like torn pieces of flesh in their huge mandibles. Gross.

Wait... Mandibles. Oh no, it can't be. I open my mouth... The stick drops.

I'm an ant? How did this happen? Yes, I am definitely one of them. I can feel my extremities. Six legs. A large backside segment. Antennae in front of my face. I have the same array of unmoving eyes on each side of my head.

How did I get here? I must be in the nest of these creatures. Or, *my* nest, I suppose.

I finally become sobered to the reality surrounding me. I slowly begin to recall my experiences of the recent days. Were they days? How did I get on this journey? Have I lost my mind? Am I... Dead? If I am, I guess I've been bad, because this must be hell. It isn't exactly what I would envision as heaven.

Ow! Hey, watch where you're going! What am I saying? I'm trying to communicate with giant ants! I need to go back to sleep so I can wake up back in my bed. Oh, how I wish I was back home! I hope I'm not dead. I need another chance to live my life better than I have been.

It's no good. There is no way I can sleep in this environment. Maybe if I could get out of this hell and find some peace I could manage it. It seems like I'm going to have to sleep to ever escape. I've had some strange experiences, but this is awful. I had felt panicked by claustrophobia, but now I'm feeling better. I won't say comfortable, but tolerable.

So, I'm still an ant. It's bad enough to wake up and find yourself in a whole new world, but being slammed into it in a state of amnesia is cruel!

Uh, but I'm feeling better now. Yes, this is a fascinating place. If I am dead, something is guiding me on this voyage. This multi-vision is amazing. It's a bit overwhelming to try to process it all, though. I couldn't see this clearly before. I now find myself at a strange balance between disgust and interest. Now that I realize I'm still an ant in the nest, I feel safe.

What are those white things? I must move forward a bit for a better look. I can hardly work my legs. I don't really need to, though. I keep getting pushed further in.

I take a couple of halting steps and get slammed forward. Ugh! The white things are larvae of ants! Their writhing is nauseating. Yuck!

Yes, and the ants passing in carry food, and those passing out do not. I remember now. What a horrible place! This is disgusting! I see a bit of a space around the corner. I might as well move forward a bit. It's difficult to coordinate these legs.

Ouch! Don't hit me! Watch where you're going! Oh my, what a hideous sight... The queen! She is so massive and bulbous. Ugh, I think she is laying eggs. I'm going to be sick... I must get out of this place. But which way to go? Oh yes, of course. I must follow the ants moving away from here.

But how do I do that? There's a never-ending stream moving in that I must cross. I would cause a tremendous pile-up of bodies. I can't be trapped here.

Ugh... What do I do? Ah, yes, those passing in must find a place to turn about. I should follow them. Yes, they have to come back out. Ugh, this is not going to be easy. I can't seem to coordinate my legs properly. Okay, I can certainly control them individually. I must get the hang of this... One step at a time... Ow! Hey! Move around! Don't push!

Take a step. Okay, now take another. Step. Ugh. Ow! Watch it! Step, step, step. Okay, I'm getting better. Step, step. Uh, try again. Step, step, step. Step, two, three four. Yes. Step, two, three, four.

Oh, the sheer volume of this space around the queen is staggering. More eggs than I can possibly count. More larvae than I can possibly count. A never-ending stream of ants. The efficiency is certainly admirable.

>»∗∗∗«

Ugh, my head. I begin to untangle the complex of signals coming in. I can smell the food. I don't know if smell is the right word. I can sense it. I can sense the queen. Yes, she has a most appealing aura about her. Yes, it is quite potent. Oh my, she is a most beneficent and admirable Queen! She is the most important being in the whole world. The most beautiful being in the universe. I must serve her. I must devote my very existence to her!

Oh, the place is a wonder. I can sense direction... I can sense a path leading to where I should go. Yes, there is the turn. There is where the others turn and start a new mission for food. I see the younglings developing. They will make most excellent servants to the colony. They will continue what we do now forever onward. I see the birthing of babies. What a beautiful sight. Ah, the security of order – the benefit of a single purpose.

Yes, I must follow the path. I must gather food for the colony. I must serve the Queen!

I follow the path through many twists and turns. I've not yet mastered the coordination of my legs, and many have passed me, but I continue on.

I sense a choice coming. Yes, two paths are becoming distinct. I will choose this one. Yes, here we go. I will follow this path. This food source is more urgent and must be collected before it is lost to the colony. Ah, I think I've got the hang of this now. It's difficult to coordinate walking on six legs.

I follow along the path and come to the outside. My, what an amazing sight. The grass grows like great trees. I can see warm afternoon light flicker between the great strands as they cross and become dense above.

I can see to the front, to the sides, somewhat to the rear – and all points between in a discrete continuum of images.

Hmm. I sense something. Yes. I can *hear*. Actually, it wouldn't properly be called hearing.

I can *understand*, but the communication is not separated into words. I just understand. Meaning is broadcast into my head. Yes, it says the threat on this path has passed on and it is now safe. We must gather the food with haste. Priority has been placed on this path. Yes, I felt that before. The message is much simpler than that. It takes a number of words to convey in English.

We continue weaving about the grass. Hmm, there has been some disturbance here. There is much bending and breaking of the grass stalks. Ugh, and the fading sense of a past battle. Oh my, yes, I can see the bodies of dead comrades. I was here before.

Yes, there is no more noble way to give one's life than in the service of the Queen. We all have a singular purpose. Ah. I can sense the food source coming. It was a flying beast of some sort. Yes, here we go. Climb in, grab on, rip. Yes, I have a handsome piece of flesh.

Now, back to the Queen! I turn and retrace my steps all the way back to the vicinity of the Queen and drop off my load. Yes, nothing is more satisfying than having a singular goal and continuing to achieve it.

As you can tell, being an ant is an engrossing experience. In every march along a path to food there's a song. It's difficult to explain it in human terms. As I described before, ants do not communicate in words. Any communication between two ants is not explicit. The song isn't entertainment. It's inspirational, I would say. It's a reflection of the love of community.

I can't really distinguish if I'm singing along with the song, or just hearing it. It seems like a combination of the two. I can't convey the experience exactly, but here is something that I think captures the feeling:

> *Out, out, out we go,*
> *to serve our Queen below!*
> *Go, go, go for food,*
> *return to feed the brood!*
> *On, on, on we move,*
> *to do what we must do!*
> *Fight! Fight! Fight! We fight,*
> *to defend what is right!*
> *Out, out, out we go,*
> *to serve our Queen below!*

That is a woefully brief replica of what I'm experiencing. There are an unlimited number of unique verses, but I don't have the talent to approach the beauty and complexity of it. I hope you can at least begin to imagine what it's like. It's a very inspirational experience.

I continue to follow down to the turning point. Then I head back away from the Queen.

Oh, this has been a long day. I am in need of rest. I believe I can rest now. It's time to move on. I must take a different path. Yes, here it is. This is a path to a resting area.

I continue on, taking various turns through quite a number of intersections, until I come to a tunnel which leads to a broader open area. Yes, this is where I can find rest.

I pass around the perimeter of the resting area until I find an open cove. Yes, this will do nicely. I step in and curl up into a warm and comfortable spot.

As hyper and immersive an experience being an ant is, I immediately go to sleep, and that is the last I remember of that place and time.

13............. *Even Smaller*

I wake up to... Violence! The world around me is erupting! What is that infernal commotion? Ugh... It's like an earthquake! Where am I? It's dark. I can't see a thing.

I try to feel around to see where I am. This is definitely not home. It feels like I'm in a cave. I try to focus and gather my senses. Maybe the incessant shaking is clearing my head faster than usual, but now I remember faster than before the adventure I had been on.

This is clearly different from yesterday. Or, I guess it was yesterday. I'd chatter my teeth out of my head for this quaking if I had any teeth.

Wait, do I have teeth? I don't think I do. Well, no, of course I'm not myself again this morning. Is it morning? It feels like I slept this time. Now it feels like I've slept half of the next day away as well.

Ugh, where am I and what am I now? Will this never end? Still, it has been quite an experience. I begin to eagerly anticipate what adventure I'll have now.

I really can't see a thing. I seem to have been starting this way recently. This time I can't sense at all what's happening around me, except the rumbling is driving me mad!

Wait, I *can* sense something. The air is stuffy. I'm enclosed somewhere. Yes, I thought that before. This is not normal. No, this is not normal at all. I must get out!

Yes, yesterday, if it was yesterday, I woke up as an ant. I had a couple of adventures, and then something unusual happened. My consciousness returned to me right at the heart of the nest. What a frightening experience it was!

Ugh, the rumbling is nauseating. I gather myself again to think. Yes.

I found myself with a clear head in close vicinity to the queen, and then something even more unusual happened. I began to feel at home. It was as if I was transitioning back into an ant, but now I remained conscious through the process.

Plus, I was able to see clearly through the segmented eyes. I can't begin to fully explain what *that* was like! Initially it's disorienting to be able to see in so many slightly different directions at the same time, but once you get used to it it's like… It's like… Well, if humans see in 3-D, it's like seeing in 99-D. Truly mind-blowing.

》✳✳✳《

Right, back to yesterday. Yes. I continued on until I went to sleep. I went to sleep in that large chamber.

I again steel myself against the incessant rumbling around me. Okay. I've been waking in close proximity to where I slept, and every time I've been a smaller creature. Given the rumbling and stuffy environment, I must still be in the ant nest. I believe I'm still in the sleeping area.

Oh, my. What am I now if I'm not an ant? What is smaller than an ant? Will they eat me? I must be in great peril.

But, what's worse is I can't see at all. I must either not have eyes or my eyes don't work in here. Yes, I feel I must get outside. My eyes must work better outside if I have any.

There's nothing for it. I must attempt to exit the nest. Who knows how far down I am, and if I'm as small as I feel it's going to be a tremendously long way to go to get out.

Well, I must go. I must be careful to not be seen. I have no doubt I'll be killed if I'm seen, and there's not much place to hide once I'm in the main chamber of this area.

As I progress I notice no creature passing near me. Yes, of course, the ants must all be out foraging. The rest area must be completely vacant except for me.

I carefully find my way to the opening to the tunnel that leads to the exit. I can't begin to convey how violent the situation is – an endless stampede of giant ants rumbling by. How can I get through this?

I no longer fear at this point of being seen. I simply must try to get out no matter what. My chief concern is being trampled. Actually, I feel quite brave.

I imagine how I would have handled being in a position like this in the real world. Or, I suppose it was the real world. Will I ever return? Do I want to return?

Yes, I want to return. There is no limit to the possibility as a human of what you can do, what you can become. Was I taking advantage of this wonderful opportunity?

Maybe in some ways I was, but I must say I had been too caught up in things that really don't mean much in the sum-total of life. I hope I can go back and make amends. I must especially be a better husband and friend to Sharon. She has always supported me, even though she has come to agree with me less and less.

Come to think of it, why was I arguing with her? It all seems pointless now. Oh yes, I do hope I will have another chance. Will I ever make it back?

This experience has really opened my eyes so-to-speak. The life of a mouse is so free, such an adventure. It was not exactly care-free, but certainly less full of care than the real world. There are responsibilities that must not be ignored, though. There are duties that must be accomplished – much like the ants. Yes, responsibilities must be pursued with dedication.

I now think of these things standing at the threshold of my destruction. If I die here, is it the end? I can feel the gigantic ants rumble down the tunnel, but can see nothing.

I would worry frequently about my safety in the real world, about attacks from enemies unseen. How absurd. There are real threats in the world. You must not waste your time being paralyzed in fear when you can't even see a threat. You must properly identify what actually is a threat.

»∗∗∗«

I try to think back. Yes, I believe this tunnel goes in one direction – out. That will be helpful. I can't risk following in deeper. There is already too far to go to get out. I must get out.

I can definitely feel that the ants are going from right to left. Yes, that is the way out. If I can manage to follow their path I will come to the outside. Once I'm out of the nest and out of their path they will not be a danger to me. Oh, but I'm likely to be so much slower than them. How will I not be crushed?

Ah… yes. I believe it is possible. I'm certain the movement of the ants is very regular. Yes, it is. Rhythm is what ants are all about. I believe if I pace myself in phase with them I can move between the footfalls of two of the ants and not be crushed. Yes, there must be a certain number of steps I can take between each step of the ants.

I stand there for a long while attuning myself to the marching of the ants. I gain some concept of how fast they go, how frequently the feet land, and what speed I should go to get in phase with them.

Yes, I believe I have identified a speed I can go that will work. I finally become quite confident, and feel for an initial route to follow to be up to speed once I enter the path. I step back and practice passing by the opening.

Yes, I can do this. I still can't see, but I can feel. Okay. In position. Ready, set, go!

I speed into the stream. Oh my... I can feel the heavy footfalls around me. Yes, they are very predictable. But this is very scary. Okay. I think it's working. I can still remember being one of them, and the rhythm of the march. It's working. Stay focused. I hope I can hold out. There's a very, very long way to go.

I won't bore you with the details of this process, but after a weary long time and various grazing blows that leave me beaten and frazzled, I finally feel the open air. I shoot out of the nest with the march and shuffle sideways away from them.

Whew! I made it!

≫ ✳ ✳ ✳ ≪

I can see! Well, not really. I can't see clearly at all. I apparently don't have eyes like an ant. I can only see in one direction, and that looks very fuzzy. I can see light. I can make out the vague shapes of passing ants nearby. Their marching is terribly noisy. Actually, I can't hear. I can feel the vibrations. Imagine a thousand soldiers running in unison, and that might approximate it. Oh yeah, and imagine them all being fifty feet tall. Yeah, that's what it's like.

I sense around me and identify a grass stalk. Oh my, the trunk is like a redwood! No, it's much bigger than that. Wow. I walk over to it and begin to climb.

Oh yes, I'm good at this. I'm good at climbing plants. I must go higher. Yes, something is telling me to go higher. Ugh, my battered body. At least I'm alive.

I climb up the stalk. I climb up and find a blade of grass branching out. I follow the blade up and up. Wow, this is like climbing a tower. Or better, it's like climbing a tower in zero gravity with spiked boots. Yeah, that's what it's like.

Whoa! The grass is swaying in the wind. Hey, no problem. My grip is like glue. I can hold on through anything. I climb up the underside of the grass blade to get some shelter from the wind.

I feel I must seek a plant higher up than grass. Yes, my home is close. I climb higher and higher. I can sense something. Yes, that's my destination. I navigate between grass stalks where the great blades cross. I do this a number of times and cover what was a tremendous distance to me, though maybe actually only a few inches in actuality.

Yes, this is it. I follow a grass blade that touches the trunk of my destination plant. I cross over onto the trunk. Ah yes, the sweet smell of my host plant. This is my home. I follow the trunk far, far up to a branch where I sense a familiar smell.

I follow this branch for a long way. Yes, this is the smell where feeding occurs.

I follow the smell and it leads me to a smaller branch and onto a leaf. Home! Yes, this is home. My people are here.

14............   *A Day in the Life, Part 4*

At this point I must intercede and provide some information. I joined my family and began feeding on the leaf. That is all we did. A leaf was a vast space to one of that kind, and we didn't finish that one leaf in my whole time there. I could not identify what I was at the time, but I can describe what I saw.

I afterward learned from a botanist from my description that what I was is called a spider mite. I believe the plant of my clan was located in a small garden in the back yard. The anthill must have been very close to the garden. A spider mite, I am told, is typically about half a millimeter in length.

They are called spider mites because they spin webs. They don't use these webs for capturing creatures to eat, but rather to build protective structures, like beds. This is probably because there are no bugs smaller than a spider mite, though I didn't think to ask the botanist if there are. I can't imagine that there could be.

After a weary long time of incrementally consuming from the leaf, I had a similar experience to what I had as an ant. Thankfully it was the part after the shock. I retained my own consciousness and it seemed to gradually merge with the consciousness of the mite. I return now to the description of what I experienced from that point forward.

»***«

This is a visually stunning environment. My kind is a vivid color of red that contrasts brilliantly with the green of the leaf. We have a body somewhat like that of a tick, with four sets of legs. The body is covered with thick, conical, white hairs. The foremost legs are used somewhat like arms – they extend more straightforward than the other three pairs, and are used to manipulate. We also have a short pair of legs (or mandibles) at the mouth. We have two small, widely-separated eyes. They functioned poorly before, but now I see very clearly.

We spend all of our time incrementally consuming nutrition from the leaf. The curiosity I gained about this wore off quite quickly. We are so close to the leaf that the smallest subdivisions of its construction are clear. It's an endless myriad of cells.

I feed on one cell at a time, consuming all that it can provide. After one is finished, I move on to the next. The number of such cells on a leaf is uncountable. I have no idea how long it takes to consume an average-sized leaf, but we've only covered a small part of one leaf in the time I've been here.

One interesting thing we do is spin a sort of silk thread. I suppose we must be some obscure (and tiny) family of spiders.

As we feed, there is a sudden jolting movement. The entire plant shakes quite violently. Of course we can hold on through this, and everyone continues feeding as if nothing happened.

I grow quite weary of the incessant feeding after a long while, and I decide to strike out on my own and do some exploring. It seems plain that the others are disturbed at this behavior, but they don't hinder me or attempt to follow. They just keep feeding.

I walk off of the leaf onto its branch. The branch it attaches to is relatively small, so I decide to head back to the trunk to find a more significant branch of the plant. There would be more opportunity to find something to do on a big branch.

I go up a bit on the trunk and quickly find a branch that's too large to fathom. I cover all sides of it and I guess it's not much smaller in diameter than the trunk. I cover quite a length of it, and then notice right before a diverting branch it slopes significantly downward. I perceive there must be a great weight hanging from this branch. So, I follow the branch down, and shortly I find myself on a relatively smooth, red surface.

Given the characteristics of this plant, even though at this scale it's quite a different world, I believe it's a tomato plant. It must be the tomato plant in the back garden.

The tomato I'm standing on is impossibly large. I can barely make out the curvature of it when looking at the horizon. Yes, this is quite a fascinating position to be in.

I then realize the jolting of the plant I felt previously must have been due to a tomato being picked from it. I hope no one will come to pick the one I'm standing on!

The thought is terrifying, so I quickly make my way back to the trunk. If this is a tomato plant, there's not much more to be seen other than more of the same. I get the feeling if I explore too much I might get more than I'm willing to bargain for, anyway.

I decide now to play around with my web-making ability. I haven't tried it myself yet. I have to trust my instincts to get a thread started, because my eyes are not capable of examining my own body. I manage to figure out by feel how to attach a web to the branch I'm standing on.

I won't go into detail of what it feels like I'm doing – I'll just say it's not terribly glamorous. I can feel the resistance of the thread as it's drawn from me.

I begin to walk around the perimeter of the branch, drawing out a long thread. I walk all the way around and indeed form a full loop, reaching back to the original end.

I wonder if I could hang from it like a spider. Thankfully before I go dangling I think to first attempt a test. I attempt to draw back on the thread while standing on the branch. I can't do it.

I feel I would be in a terribly uncoordinated position if I hang from a thread and attempt to pull my way back up, so I think better of it. If I strand myself dangling I would have to hope to be able to sleep to have any chance of escaping this adventure, and that would be difficult to do in such a position.

My brain boggles for a moment at the thought that my *real* life might actually be at risk.

»****«

Have you ever tried to think of what nothingness is like? For existence to have never happened? Have you ever been able to detach your thinking from reality so that for some brief moment there really is nothingness? That's what I feel like now.

And then my brain snaps back and it's like it jumps to the opposite pole and I feel disoriented. Then again this whole experience has been like that over and over again. What will happen next? Will I keep getting smaller? Isn't there a point that can't be divided? What then?

»****«

I return my thinking to my current situation again, and I tie off the thread and decide to go try something else. This is fairly fun so I should just make the most of it. I also won't go into detail about how it feels a thread is terminated. That's not too glamorous either.

I then move to a very small branch that's sprouting from a high part of the trunk. I tie a thread to it and then to the trunk. I then tie a thread to that one and tie it over to another nearby branch. I play around with this for a while, forming something like a spider web, but not a very good one I'm afraid. Too bad I wasn't an actual spider in this adventure. At least it seems I'm heading in a direction where I won't get any bigger, and there are no spiders that are smaller than this!

I then move to a small leaf growing out of the small branch, and completely wrap it in web. I realize I'm pretty good at that. I can mummify quite well.

I decide this is the end of my explorations. I go back to the trunk and make my way down toward the branch to the home leaf.

Unfortunately I'm in for some more excitement. As I approach where the branch to the home leaf joins the trunk, I see a massive shape moving on one side of the trunk.

I stand frozen in terror, unable to comprehend what it might be. It continues to move, and I begin to realize it's moving toward me. It comes closer and closer. The dimension of it is mind-boggling. It's as big to me as the car was in the garage as a mouse. Yes, in case you didn't figure it out, that was Sharon's car that ran over Nib's tail. I wonder how he's doing.

I can't believe what I'm seeing. The vast shape writhes as it approaches. It's making the whole tomato plant shake violently – at least the parts near to it. I quickly gather my wits and move backward up the trunk. I see another side branch, and step onto it.

I hope the beast doesn't decide to follow me! I have no way to defend myself!

I try to hide behind the branch as the beast approaches, but I also peek around to see just what this gargantuan creature is. I can see the massive head approach, followed by an impossibly bulky body.

I can't begin to tell you how hideous the face of this creature is – much uglier than an ant. And its head is the size of a barn!

Luckily it doesn't bother with me, if it even sees me, and it keeps moving up the trunk past the branch I'm hiding behind. I can feel the branch vibrate as it passes.

I can now see it has a myriad of legs like a centipede down the bulky body, but much less than a hundred of them. Great waves pass up the body as the feet step forward one after another, grasping around the trunk. The body seems like it's a mile long. It takes forever to pass.

Of course! It's a caterpillar! Wow, it is such a horrible thing to see this close. I must be very small indeed. I wonder what kind of beautiful flying creature that caterpillar will turn into. It must be heading up the plant to feed on leaves itself.

After the beast is well past, I step back onto the trunk behind it. Its vast bulk wraps around a good portion of the massive trunk. What a ponderous beast.

I turn and make my way back to the home leaf, taking in the sights as I go. You don't get perspective like this every day. I wish I had better appreciated it when I was an ant. When I was a cricket. When I was a mouse. When I was a cat. When I was a… human.

It's quite amazing to be able to climb such a massive tree and walk upside-down, sideways, whatever.

I eventually find my way back to the home leaf. I arrive to find all the others are comfortably tucked away in their beds. We don't have any advanced form of communication, but it would have been nice to have hung out a bit more, so to speak.

I find that a comfy-looking bed is left unoccupied. No doubt it's mine. It makes quite a warm and inviting pouch. I snuggle in and drink in the environment for a long time, enjoying the simplicity of this existence. Still, I think it would be nice to get away. It's one of those things that are fun to do once, but become a chore the more you do it. I don't suppose they feel that way, though. I've spent some time in their mindset, if you follow me, and there isn't much of a demand there for a broader range of things to do.

It seems the smaller you get the more boring life is. I find myself actually conflicted now in what I hope to have happen when I next awake. Maybe this is the end of the adventure. Whatever happens, I want to make the most of it.

Eventually the fatigue of another long day overcomes my wonder of living in this world, and that is the last I remember of that place and time.

15............ A Different State of Being

My next state of consciousness is much more like a dream, though like no dream I've ever had before or since. My brain couldn't possibly invent such an existence.

I feel awake, but I don't have senses at all comparable to human ones. There isn't any such complexity. I'm conscious, but not much more than that. If I had not had the experience of the last few days, if they were days, I would be very confused. Instead, it's immediately obvious to me that I'm not back to being human yet, that is certain.

Somehow, in spite of my now simplistic existence, I can remember and think normally. I feel myself among many others like me. I'm aware that I could move if my environment was flexible enough. Though there is no sense of controlling it, I can tell that my movement is generated from my body like swimming.

My sole purpose of existing is to grow. I continuously consume from the environment around me, as if I absorb food. I realize at some extent of size that my body splits into two.

Yes, that's what I said. And at some point through the split I can sense that the *other* part is not me anymore. It goes its own way and I do not further concern myself with it. I am then half the size I was, and the whole process starts again. It's an endless loop.

One peculiar aspect of this splitting is every once in a while I can recognize some degree of difference in the other part from myself. It's still of me, but not identical to me.

And the concept of time seems to have changed. All at once it seems like a normal amount of time is passing while also feeling like it's a million years.

I have no senses other than those described. Beyond that I only sense one particular change of situation that occurs. That is going from a fairly static existence to a more fluid existence, to a very fluid existence, and back to a more static existence.

»✳✳✳«

I must interject at this point to provide more information. As long as I existed this way, I had no clue what was going on. I was afraid this was what it was like to die, and eventually there would be nothing. I became very afraid that I would eventually become stuck forever in nothingness. I could definitely sense a simpler existence. Given the previous transitions of state, to progressively smaller creatures, I figured I must have been some being that is smaller and simpler than a mite. I discussed this subject with the botanist previously mentioned, and he directed me to a biologist.

Please note that the questions I asked of the biologist (and the other specialists that I consulted) were not phrased as if I had experienced these things first-hand, though I will phrase it that way here for consistency. Obviously if I had said I had been a cat and a mouse and so forth they would have either laughed me out of their offices or called the authorities or both!

This biologist, after hearing the full tale, deduced from my description that I must have been some sort of single-celled organism. Given that my transitions up to that point were to an organism not far distant from the previous one, she surmised that this time I must have been somewhere on the tomato plant. Her best guess from my description was that I was a bacteria cell on the surface of a tomato, eating away at it.

She told me that such a bacterium has what is called a flagellum at one end, which acts as a propeller, and it uses it to move in a fluid environment. It uses oxygen to process the sugar of the tomato to make energy, and thereby grow. I did not understand this concept at that time, but I can say it does not seem contrary to my experience.

She then surmised that my perception of moving from static to liquid to static sounded like the common process by which a bacterium spreads. She suggested that I was among a colony on one tomato (or possibly somewhere else), and by a raindrop or accumulated condensation I swam into that liquid and then fell or splashed onto another tomato. The liquid then dried, leaving me back in a static state where I continued to multiply. She informed me the difference I recognized between myself and the *daughter cell*, as she described the cell that split from me, is called a 'mutation'. She said this is a primary component of the Theory of Evolution.

I had previously found this concept to be hard to imagine, and I expressed as much to the biologist. She proceeded to describe for me that it is theorized that mutations also occur in higher organisms, such as animals, and sometimes a mutation proves to be beneficial and increases the chances of survival of that organism. This is called Natural Selection, another fundamental component of the Theory of Evolution. She explained that this is a very slow process and takes an amount of time to show results that is beyond the common conception of humans, who only live for a number of decades. I thought this theory sounded interesting for a bacteria cell, but for humans?

When I first heard the theory of the biologist that I was a bacterium, I found the news to be disappointing. I had transitioned between being different parasites of the tomato plant – mites and infection – a most humbling realization. The biologist then informed me that there would be no life at all on Earth without bacteria. It was the first form of life, and all organisms derived from it, eventually to humans.

This news certainly put things in a different perspective, but it's difficult to imagine humans descending from bacteria. I asked her how exactly humans could descend from a single-celled organism. She reminded me that the process took millions of years, if the theory is correct, and there were many stages of development. From one cell to many, to specialized multi-celled organisms, to fish-like creatures, to water creatures that adapted to living on land, and onward to mammals and to humans, a type of mammal. I guess it's *possible*.

16.............   *Further In*

From this point onward my experience became less distinct. In fact, I cannot say how long the whole process endured. Time began to change meaning. Or, at least it seemed to from my perspective. I consulted a physicist who attempted to explain to me that there is a relation between time and space. I had to stop him as he was explaining in terms that I could not follow, and then he summarized as follows:

"If you were always of a size, you would not know anything different than the pace of time you were used to. But, supposing you were to become progressively smaller, you would perceive time to move progressively slower compared to what you were used to. If you were familiar with how long a second lasted, you would perceive the length of the same amount of time to grow longer as you grew smaller."

Reflecting on this, I believe it makes sense. As a mouse, humans appeared extremely slow-moving to me. The cat was faster than humans, but still slower than a mouse. And the sound of the cat roaring at me was deeper and slower than how it sounds to human ears.

The further I went, the less I could describe, and the more I needed a theory from someone smarter than myself to explain it. For the sake of simplicity, I will continue with the information subsequently gained from scientists integrated with my descriptions.

»✳✳✳«

I could not explain what was happening as I saw it. There were a few moments that I had some clue, but for the most part it was an inexplicable wonder to me. I had been afraid of where I was going, but I now began to become overwhelmed in fascination. If I was dead, maybe this was heaven after all.

The best explanation I have been able to find for my experience up to this point was that my consciousness somehow transferred. I transferred from a human to a cat, then to a mouse, then to a cricket, then to an ant, then to a mite, and then to a single cell. All of these transitions occurred during sleep. I went to sleep *inside* the body of one, and woke up *inside* the body of another. This transition jumped between locations that were relatively close together. I did not *return* to my body through the process, at least not consciously, and the whole thing seemed to take a number of days in total.

At this point the experience changed. Rather than *being* the cell I had been, I found myself actually inside of it. Space seemed to turn inside out, and I sensed what was inside rather than outside. I found I had become an observer rather than an occupier, you might say.

This time the transition happened consciously, rather than during sleep. My senses reduced to an awareness of the presence of other things. I wouldn't call it vision. There was no color. There was no sound. There was no touch. I just *understood* what was around me. I will equate this sensation from this point forward as *feeling* and *seeing* for the sake of simplicity.

»＊＊＊«

I feel as if I'm floating in soup. There are various shapes floating about amid a background that seems like liquid. Directly before me is what resembles an elongated pile of spaghetti. It's just suspended in the soup. From my first being aware of the transition inside, I have progressively moved closer to this spaghetti. I have no control of movement. I'm set on a course that will not deviate.

My biologist consultant informed me with a look of incredulity that I had accurately described the chromosome of the bacteria cell I had previously described. She said the inside of a bacteria cell is made up of various materials such as proteins, and at the center is what is called a circular chromosome. It is a single closed loop.

I can see now that this chromosome is closely surrounded by other objects. This central area within the cell is denser than the rest. It is called the nucleoid, and these materials surrounding the chromosome are proteins and enzymes and RNA, or ribonucleic acid. RNA is similar to DNA, or is like a subset of it. DNA means deoxyribonucleic acid. As you may know, DNA is the blueprint of genetics. It really defines what you are, whether you're a single-cell bacterium or a human, or any organism.

As I move closer to the chromosome, I can more clearly see its shape.

The loop is bunched together, but not tangled. I can now sense that the surrounding walls are beginning to close in about me.

I get close enough that I can now distinguish the texture of the string. Yes, the string is actually a spiraling ladder. This is one of the few moments of this part of the adventure where I feel I recognize what I see. I think most of us have seen what DNA looks like, or at least how it is represented in an illustration. I can confirm that the real thing is a quite similar shape.

I can now see clearly enough that this spiraling ladder is a chain of interconnected – well, balls – balls of different sizes smushed together.

Now there is movement. I see objects swimming down the ladder, and it begins to uncoil. I now see the ladder break, and it begins to unzip, you could say. No sooner does it pull apart than objects swimming around it begin to join up with the separated strands and turn them into two distinct ladders.

The broken ends of both ladders join together to reform the now independent loops and one of the ladders begins to drift away. As it does, I notice a slight difference in shapes of the elements in one part of the two ladders while all the rest seem identical. This is a mutation like that previously described by the biologist.

Yes, this is the splitting of one cell into two, and the now-becoming distinct second cell is slightly different than the original. This mutation might serve as an enabler or a disabler to that cell.

»✳✳✳«

I asked the biologist about mutations in higher organisms such as humans. We clearly do not multiply by dividing into two. Obviously we eat and grow, but we multiply by birthing. The biologist reminded me that the DNA of a child is defined by that of the mother and father. Yes, I remember that. A sperm carries the father's DNA, the egg carries the mother's DNA, and the two are combined.

She said when this happens it's more complicated than the division of a single cell, and if I had experienced that it would have been more difficult to identify a mutation. Still, mutations can occur. She said conditions such as Down's syndrome are due to identified mutations. There are many that make it more difficult for a person to survive. At the same time there are many that make it easier to survive. Usually an individual change is so small that it's not even noticeable to a human. This is quite a fascinating concept.

The biologist then went off on a rant which I thought was strange, so I'll repeat it here. While she was explaining beneficial mutations, she complained "with medicine and other modern technology, mutations have less effect. If you have a detrimental mutation, it is treated and you live longer than your ancestors would have. This defeats the benefit of Natural Selection, and therefore human beings are beginning to devolve, not evolve. At a minimum, evolution has stopped." I'm not sure what to make of this, but it sounds cruel. I hope it's not true. Wouldn't 'defective' humans have always reproduced before dying off anyway? I don't know.

»✳✳✳«

As the other ladder drifts away, I can see the outer wall closing in between. In a short time I can no longer see the other ladder, and it must have become its own chromosome in its own cell. I now realize I can distinguish texture within the elements of the ladder before me. I can generally sense that the ladder is coiling back again, but I'm so close I can only see a small portion of it, and another part of it in the distance behind. I can now see that each element that makes up the pieces of the ladder is itself segmented into smaller elements.

The biologist expressed some surprise at my description and informed me that what I had observed was the individual atoms of the chromosome. Her expression then turned to one of suspicion, and she began to grill me on my knowledge of biology and chemistry and such. I tried to explain that I didn't remember that much from school, but she accused me of being an imposter that was trying to take advantage of her. Unfortunately she refused to help me further, and ushered me out of her office. Fortunately I was able to return to the previously mentioned physicist at that point, which turned out to be appropriate.

As I get closer to one particular element, I can clearly make out spherical shapes clumped together, and each distinct element connects similarly to other elements. The physicist informed me that such a situation is due to the chemical bonding between the atoms. He went on to say that such bonding is the key to molecules and to the structure of the world in general. Yes, I think I remember that from school. It turns out to be pretty interesting stuff when you see it up close. As I move closer I can sense the attraction between the atoms.

»✳✳✳«

I must admit it is a similar feeling to electricity. You see, I would not advise attempting such a thing, but I have felt electricity. One morning I was mowing the grass with an electric mower. When I first moved into the house I received as a gift an electric mower. Unfortunately this mower did not implement a battery and needed to be attached by a cord to an outlet. The grass was wet with dew, and in order to have enough length of cord I had chained two together.

At one point I was repositioning the cords, and my hand passed over the junction between the two. The water on it was sufficient to conduct some electricity, but not enough to keep the mower from working and not enough to fry my poor body, thankfully. It was a unique situation where I could feel the electricity around the junction. It was somewhat similar to holding two like poles of a magnet together. I could feel that there was a generally spherically-shaped influence around it.

》＊＊＊《

This is similar to what I sense around the atoms, except it's like opposite poles of a magnet. They are drawn together.

I now come so close that the atoms become translucent. I can vaguely see through the shell. I continue to move closer, and I can now feel the power of the atom. I can feel it pull me, or push me, I honestly cannot tell which. Eventually I sense that I pass within the atom. I cannot conclusively say, as the closer I get the less I can see of it. I can just feel the power of it surrounding me.

The physicist, with some skepticism, said that he believed such an experience might describe passing into the electron cloud of an atom. He attempted to describe the nature of an electron to me, but I could not understand a word of it. He then generalized that an electron orbits around the nucleus of an atom, but its nature is not as tangible as a planet orbiting around the sun. You would not be able to distinguish an electron as an identifiable object, but would sense its presence. The electrons of an atom somehow occupy a spherical shape much larger than themselves all at once.

》＊＊＊《

As I pass within the influence of the electron cloud, I sense another growing power. It seems similar to that which I had already sensed, but it's in opposition. This presence gradually grows, but remains far weaker than the electron cloud.

The physicist explained that if such a situation were to be experienced, I must have sensed the presence of the nucleus. He proceeded to explain that the nucleus of an atom contains protons which are positively charged, and this charge counters that of the electrons, which are negative. He said the influence of the protons was much smaller than that of the electrons because the nucleus is in the center of the atom, and I must have been nearer to the outside. He said if you compared the size of an apple to that of the earth, the nucleus would have the same relationship in size to the extent of the atom. Yes, that would be far away indeed.

Given the physicist's description I expected to next encounter the nucleus. I must say that he became very interested to hear a description of what would happen next. It seemed that the nucleus of this atom was my destination, as the atom had been, as the element in which the atom resided had been, as the chromosome had been, as the bacteria had been, and so on. I am sorry to say that the physicist was disappointed. As for me it's difficult to express, since the reality of these things is beyond my reason, and this turned out by far to not be the end of the wonders of this journey.

》＊＊＊《

As I pass further within the atom, the strength of the nucleus grows greater. I also realize I can no longer see anything. There is only darkness. Then there is a change. My sensation of the presence of the electrons and protons gradually fades away. There is nothing.

17............   *Far Out!*

Nothing. Truly, nothing. The utter absence of anything at all. Do you remember my mentioning imagining this before? Little did I know then that I would not only experience such a thing mentally, but physically as well.

No sight, no sound, no smell, no touch. There is no time. There is no distance. Nothing has ever existed. Try to imagine how this would feel – for there to be nothing, for time to have no meaning, for space to have no meaning, and you are there to realize it. You exist, and that is all. You have no body, just a presence. Nothing will happen. Nothing ever has happened. There is nothing to happen. There never has been anything to happen. There never has been a place for anything to happen.

Can you understand how it feels? My previous fear has come true. I had lost that fear in the wonder of the experience until I reached this point of nothingness. It seems as though the entire life of the universe clicks by second after second. I am truly terrified that it will never end. Yet somehow it does end. In an instant it all changes.

»✳✳✳«

I see light. Hope returns. I see an infinitesimally small, yet infinitely bright, point of light. This is different from what I had sensed previously. This is vision. But, it is not by human eyes. My actual eyes could not endure this light, and I have no control over where I look. As before, my path seems predetermined. At the same time, I have the distinct feeling that time is moving. It had come to a stop before, and now it's moving again. Then there is another change, and from here, I fear there is no going back.

»✳✳✳«

The point of light rapidly expands to fill all vision with infinite brightness. Fear is replaced by awe. I now have the feeling that I've died and gone to heaven, and I accept it. I even welcome it. After some time the solid light fades to distinct lines radiating from the center. These lines gradually diminish in number. The remaining lines then slowly wane to individual points of light continually radiating from the center. The pace of the emanating of the points gradually slows, and the number of moving ones decreases, until the entire field of view is filled with stationary points of light.

»✳✳✳«

Well within the process of this last stage it became evident that I was looking at the night sky. The star formations were clearly familiar. How my consciousness moved from the atom to there I cannot say. Every scientist I consulted refused to speculate on what occurred between the point where I felt the presence of the atom and the point where the light appeared. I suspect they were also reluctant to diagnose what they did not already know. They seemed to be more comfortable with explaining what they did know, and I do appreciate the help they gave me.

With the lack of information, all I can describe is my own perception of what I experienced. I would say this is the ultimate example of the transitions I made. A human is relative to a cat, is relative to a mouse, and so on. A universe is relative to an atom. They are both mostly empty space. Our universe could be among an infinite number of universes, like atoms of a greater organism. That's what it felt like – like space and time turned in on each other. Impossibly small became impossibly large, and time started over from the Beginning.

»✳✳✳«

As I stare at the starry sky, a star that seems to be at the very center twinkles. It gradually waxes until it looks like it's burning, and its color becomes golden. After a time more points of light begin to emanate from this fiery point. The first few are faint and fly by quickly. Then a point flies by more slowly and becomes a brilliant blue. It grows slightly in size as it passes. The next point flies by yet slower, becoming a pale blue, and it grows as it passes as well. Shortly another point flies by. It's yellowish and rapidly grows as it passes.

This is another part of the journey where I can say I recognize what I see. As this point grows and flies by, it grows so large that I recognize it as the planet Saturn with its grey rings. I even see a glint of a moon or two about it. Next comes Jupiter. It grows so large as it passes by that I can clearly distinguish the colored bands of its surface. Again I catch the glints of a few of the moons of this great planet. A band of points of light occupying the full field of view from left to right then wax into view and diverge away from the center until they're out of view. This is the asteroid belt.

After the asteroid belt of course is Mars, and as it waxes rusty red and passes I can see the texture of its surface. Through this whole process the fiery object at the center, clearly our Sun, has continued to slightly grow in size. Then a speck appears in the center of the Sun. The speck grows into a black spot until it eclipses the Sun, leaving a fantastic halo. At this point the Sun begins to move and the black spot, which we know to be our Earth, remains in the center. As the Sun illuminates the Earth, the brilliance and beauty of our blue home is beyond awe-inspiring.

At this point I notice the glint of the Moon. It gradually moves below the Earth as it all comes closer. I see the shadow of the Earth growing upon the Moon, causing its shape to appear to change into an upward-pointing crescent. As the Earth grows larger I can distinguish cloud patterns and the hint of land below the atmosphere. The moon passes out of view before I can see any great detail. Shortly I can distinguish the familiar shape of the Americas. The Earth then rapidly rushes at me, and I recognize that I'm heading in the general area of Texas, where I live.

In a second I expect to land, but that is the last I remember of that perspective.

18............   *The Next Day*

I wake up. Light shines through the window. I don't move for a long time, my mind not being used to the sensations I feel. I realize I'm breathing. I begin to remember the sensation of touch, feeling the bed under me and being aware of my extremities. I begin to remember the sensation of hearing, hearing my own breathing and the chirps of birds outside. I realize I exist, and the environment becomes familiar.

Yes, I am Rupert Michael, and this is my home. I am lying on my own bed.

I rise slightly and look at the alarm clock. It is there. Eight in the morning, Saturday. I look over to the other side. Sharon lies there sleeping.

After all I've experienced I must say my first feeling is melancholy. Is the journey over? Do I have to go back so soon? My second feeling is disappointment. I know in my heart the journey *is* over. I will be myself from now on. I will never have more adventures with Nib.

I wonder what feeling I might have the next time I see a mouse. I chuckle at the thought that my first reaction would likely be to jump in fear. I don't know the last time you saw a mouse, but it is frightening at first sight. At least it is for me.

What would I think? Is it Nib? Is it Rit? Could it even be Tib? Could it be a cub of theirs or one of a long line of descendants? A mouse only lives a couple of years.

What is it thinking about me, one of those blundering humans? I chuckle again. I know I am a true threat to them. Yes, but they will carry on and live free regardless of what threatens them.

My third feeling is alienation. What would I want to be if I had the choice? Would I rather be a human, a cat, a mouse, a cricket? An ant? No, being an ant is hard work and there's no fun to be had. I chuckle again.

I lay long and think back on my experience. No, I want to be me. I realize again how fortunate I am to be human, what possibility is automatic as a human. I am capable of making of my life what I want it to be. I can make a difference in the lives of not just people, but any living being, even the Earth itself. After all I experienced, my view of life has utterly changed.

»****«

I can say with as much certainty as exists in my life that when I awoke that morning it was reality. I have had no *out of body* experiences since then. I had gone on a journey, and now it was complete. I turn toward Sharon, who sleeps facing me. I watch her breathe. She has a look of tranquility on her face.

She may be dreaming of escape to a happy life, or maybe return to a previous state of happiness. I will do what I can to make her happy from now on. I remember what I saw in her face that I fell in love with years before. How have I gone so long without recalling that feeling?

As I lay there and allow myself to become immersed in my love for Sharon like I haven't since very early in our relationship, she opens her eyes. I smile to watch her transition from sleep into consciousness. No doubt the fact that I'm smiling at her contributes to her confusion.

She's initially annoyed. "What are *you* smiling at?" she asks. I speak with body language as I move close to her and move my face to hers. She gradually succumbs and we kiss.

She then smiles in shock and asks "what has gotten into you?" I can tell she realizes this is not mere friskiness.

"I'm just happy to be with you," I say.

She sits up and becomes serious, saying "I can't remember the last time you said something like that."

"I love you," I say.

She stares at me in silence for a moment, and a tear wells in her eye. "I love you too," she says, and the tear rolls down her cheek.

Tears come to my eyes too, and she lays down on me with her head on my chest. I wrap my arms around her. I can feel a tear or two splash on my chest, and I begin to cry as well. I think she felt a tear fall on her head, and she wipes her eyes, sniffles, and raises her head.

We look more deeply into each other's eyes than I can ever remember. She smiles, another tear rolls down her cheek, and she lays her head back down on my chest. I wipe the tears from my eyes, wishing to be past the pain from years of neglect that is being released from both of us. This only allows the tears to flow more voluminously. Still, tears of joy are a wonderful thing. I know the pain I have caused Sharon is draining away and I have a fresh chance to make it better from this day forward.

We lay there for a long time. I can't say how long. It doesn't matter what time it is, and if I look at the clock, the numbers have no meaning to me. All that matters is being with Sharon. Eventually the tears stop and I feel wondrously at peace. I believe with the contrast of what life had been just the day before, this is the happiest time in my life. I feel like floating on a cloud of joy.

Eventually I say "I'm hungry."

Sharon laughs. "Your stomach has been talking to me all morning."

We both laugh and the emotion of it releases more tears. She sits up and we both wipe our eyes of the fresh tears.

"Who are you and what have you done with my husband?" She places her hands on her hips and looks serious.

I smile and say "I can't explain it, but I'm a different person now."

"I think this is you. You've just buried it inside for so long."

"Yeah. I don't know why I did, but I won't do it again."

"Sounds good to me," she says, leans over to me, and we kiss again.

Yes, I certainly married the right person. I can be the right person for her, too.

"Let's go out for lunch," she says, smiles, and springs out of bed to get dressed.

I sit briefly and marvel at my good fortune. I have never felt such joy at her happiness.

Sharon pops back out of the bathroom and asks "Well, are you coming?"

I smile and get up to get dressed myself. We kiss again and I take her hand as we head out.

Our hands would remain connected for most every moment of the remainder of the day.

We enter the garage to take her car. I remember my adventure there as a mouse. I even become afraid that I might step on one, or we would drive over one. Don't worry, I tell myself. They can take care of themselves.

Unlike mine, Sharon's car fits inside the garage. Of course with the other side vacant of a vehicle, it's cluttered with boxes of a wide variety of things we've collected over the years.

Sharon drives, and I enter the passenger seat. I remember how I used to hate being in her car – how restricted I felt. This time I close the door, fasten my seat belt, and realize it's not bad at all. I guess after having squeezed through such small spaces in my journey, I now feel a sense of security in a more snug place.

As we drive around to the front of the house, I see my car parked on the curb. It's quite a shock to be reminded of how huge it is. The feeling is so foreign it's as if it had never been mine.

All I had thought of before was what was inside – how much more I got in a big car. Actually I should call it a truck. Although I've always called it a car, it's based on a truck with a luxury interior and no open bed.

The external size only meant that I occupied a higher level in the food chain, as it were. I hadn't worried myself with the waste and absurdity of effectively driving around a room of my house. I will trade that truck in for something more reasonable in short order.

»＊＊＊«

Sharon and I spent the entire day with each other, worrying about nothing. The feeling of wonder wore off over the coming days with familiarity, but we have most definitely remained just as kind to each other and happy to be together to this day with no desire to change. I will never allow myself to forget again what is really important.

»＊＊＊«

Later that day Sharon stepped out into the back yard. I hadn't done it often before, but I follow her this time. I watch as she goes out to the garden and picks a tomato. I quickly remember my experience there, and I grab the tomato from her. She stares at me in shock as I closely inspect it, trying to see if there's a mite on it. I don't see anything, but they may be too small to see.

She laughs at me and shakes her head as I hand it back to her. "What is it?" she asks.

"Oh, nothing," I say, put my hands behind my back and whistle unconcernedly.

She then goes back into the house. I look around the yard. I see the pole and birdhouse in the garden and think of my experience as the cat. I look over and see the bird bath. I look up to the ledge I had jumped off of as the mouse. Wow, that's a long drop!

I look back down at the grass and remember what it was like to look up at it from below when each stalk was like a giant tree. I then ponder where the anthill might be, and look back down to my feet. Sure enough, there's a stream of ants going across the patio. They're running in all directions, as my feet are very close to the path. I'm very scared I've stepped on some. I don't see any bodies. Whoa, I have to be more careful. I turn to carefully step back inside the house.

»✳✳✳«

That night we sat in the living room together with the TV off, talking and thinking.

Nine o'clock approaches, and Sharon says "your favorite show is coming on."

I hadn't even thought about it. I decide to go ahead and see what's on tap tonight. As I watch I gradually realize that the host is purposely trying to keep viewers on edge by stoking fear. I repeatedly look over to Sharon to see her reaction, and she only looks back with curiosity at my expression. Half-way through the show I turn off the TV. How did I fall for this nonsense before?

"You don't like it?"

I think back about how much she disliked it before, and how I used to fight with her over the various subjects. It seems so absurd now.

"I'm sorry. How did you tolerate me?"

"I tried to explain what I thought of this kind of thinking," she says, "but nothing got through. When you argue with what seems common sense, but you're shouted down, it makes you wonder what is right. It makes you afraid you're wrong. It's very depressing to think that's really the way the world works."

"I don't know what makes someone think that way. I was angry. I was frustrated. I was... Scared."

We both contemplate in silence. I realize my experience has given me perspective I didn't have before. I realize I could have been more open-minded in the past, but there's a fine line when the decision comes up, and if your thoughts are self-centered you will invariably slide down the other way. I realize I was afraid of something that was really undefinable.

I had slipped into a mode of defining my world by enemies. It was easy to see *anyone* as an enemy. My experience now makes me tend to think of what another person's perspective is – to walk in their shoes, so to speak, and not make broad judgments. I had *walked in the shoes* of a cat, a mouse, a cricket, an ant, a mite, a cell, and had traveled from the atom to the Universe.

I've determined a maxim to live my life by – that people should think more about what makes them similar than what makes them different

– then we'd all get along much better. You must have perspective – you must try to understand others. Lack of understanding makes for mistakes and injustices. This is the only way it can be if you truly believe in the Golden Rule.

Not much good can come from conducting your life by retaliating against evils you perceive done to you. You will invariably make mistakes, and then *you* become the source of evil. This is not to say that there are no enemies in the world. Making clear what a threat really is keeps you from committing injustice in the name of what you believe to be justice. When there is a fight that must be fought, you'd better make sure that's the one you're fighting. These talking heads sure won't give you a clear picture. They just want to keep you watching.

»✶✶✶«

Sharon and I talk much about such things deep into the night. We sit long in silence and ponder. Suddenly a sound comes from the dining area. Kreeeeek! Kreeeeek! Kreeeeek! It jolts my senses.

Is that who I think it is? Kreeeeek! Kreeeeek! Kreeeeek! Sharon gets up and heads in that direction.

"Just leave it," I say.

"I can't stand these annoying crickets!"

She turns on a light and the noise stops. I chuckle to think about old Krick. She turns off the light and returns to the couch. I then realize I hear another faint chirping further off. Screeeeetch, screeeeetch, screeeeetch, it sounds like.

Could it be? I realize this sound has been going for a long time but I had ignored it. I wonder if either of those boys will get lucky tonight. I chuckle again and shake my head.

"What is it?" Sharon asks.

"Nothing," I say, laughing.

She then gets up, kisses me, walks toward the bedroom, winks, and goes inside. I follow her. I won't detail how we completed the evening, as honestly, it is a private matter.

19............ *Reflections*

As I prepare for sleep I honestly do not think of having gone on my bizarre journey the previous night, and I do not consider that I could be in store for another. The world is entirely new now, and I have not directly thought about my adventure since the first part of that morning.

However when I awake the next morning I find myself unsure of where I am. After another long time of adjustment I look over and see the alarm clock. Nine o'clock, Sunday.

Yes, I'm still at home, but it takes my brain quite a while to adjust. Being a human does not necessarily seem like the most natural state to be in. This makes me ponder exactly what had occurred. I wonder *why* the experience happened. What was it that caused the journey? I was so closed-minded before. I couldn't have initiated it myself.

I still don't know the answer to that question. Maybe Sharon was right and it was inside me all along. Maybe I was due.

»∗∗∗«

As I contemplate what happened, I remember a conversation with the physicist. When I described to him what I saw when the presence of the atom faded and the light appeared, he said my description of what followed sounded like an envisioning of the Big Bang. He expressed interest in that there was a noticeable period between the point appearing and when it expanded. He was not sure what that might mean. I certainly don't know.

He surmised after much consideration that my perspective was fixed in space exactly where I lay in bed. He said it seemed that time went back to the Beginning, then the Big Bang happened and the Universe expanded through its history – the Sun formed, the Earth and other planets formed, and the whole thing moved right to me, my home and my bed moving right into its position today, the exact position I had originally been in – until that very moment when I awoke.

He explained that the Big Bang theory is based on the observation that celestial objects are generally moving further apart. This means that the universe is expanding. He said if you trace this back, it may be that the universe began at one point and has expanded from there.

The question that comes to my mind, similar to my adventure as a whole, is how did it all start? There was that point where time seemed to stop, and then... *Nothing.* Was there a point in history that nothing existed at all? Was there a point where there was no time at all? Where did all of the material of the universe come from? Where did all of the energy of the universe come from? I don't know the answer to these questions either, nor did the physicist.

He then returned to his explanation, and said it seemed that time moved infinitely fast when the point of light expanded, so that the limitless moving galaxies completely filled the field of view. As I got closer to my destination, time gradually slowed down until it reached its customary speed at the point I awoke.

This, in combination with the reduced number of galaxies passing by due to the expansion, caused the solid field to transition to lines and then to individual stars, and then those points slowed until they were relatively stationary. Once there was no more noticeable movement of stars I was within the vicinity of our solar system, and those stars were either galaxies positioned in the direction I was looking, or stars within our Milky Way galaxy. I then passed by the planets on the way to Earth, and eventually *landed* at the place and time where I awoke.

I asked the physicist why all of the galaxies looked similar to single stars in our galaxy. He explained that it was very unlikely I would pass close to any object in space on any straight line, because the distance between objects (even in the asteroid belt) is so large. Even though any galaxy is unbelievably large, they are so far apart that each one is only a point of light when looking at it from another galaxy. He said since I was going straight for it I should have seen the Milky Way expand toward me, but he supposed that the infinite count of other expanding galaxies must have cluttered the view of it.

He said even within our solar system the distance between planets is so large I was very unlikely to pass close to any of them. He thought by my description that I actually did pass relatively close to Saturn, Jupiter, and Mars, which seemed like a rare chance.

»****«

As I ponder these things, Fluffy jumps up on the bed. That has *never* happened before. He knew I didn't like him, and he avoided me. Now he jumps up and takes a look around. I reach out to stroke his head and he bounds back off. Apparently he can now sense an absence of malice on my part. I smile to think of what adventures he's heading out for.

I wonder why I disliked cats so much before – did I dislike independent thinking? I don't know. I wouldn't say that I don't like dogs now, but I definitely find people owning a dog capable of mauling even an adult to death ridiculous. The person getting mauled might very well be someone the owner cares about.

I think back to going to sleep Friday night and waking up Saturday morning after it was all over. It seemed during my experience that a number of days elapsed, but clearly it all had to have happened between Friday night and Saturday morning. Considering all the strange things I experienced, I wonder if I traveled in time. I most certainly did at the end, so why not at other times? I don't know. I can't explain it at all. My best guess is that time had a different meaning through the journey than how we normally consider it. Come to think of it, how did I not run into myself?

I then look over to Sharon. She continues to sleep peacefully. I realize that I must tell her about my experience. I will not keep secrets from her ever again, but this is not an easy thing to face. I feel ashamed that I had to be literally placed in other shoes to gain perspective. Well, of course, none of them actually wore shoes, but I trust that you get my point.

I'm terribly worried about how she will react. My behavior has already done a *one-eighty*, as the expression goes, and now if I start raving about having been her cat, a mouse, a cricket, an ant, a mite, and, and a bacterium for goodness sake – not to mention what happened after. What would she think then?

I delay telling her for many days. I puzzle over the dilemma of how to explain it. I wasn't so concerned about the reactions of the professionals I consulted. I simply wanted them to help me understand what I had seen. If they thought I was crazy, so what? Of course it's not the same with Sharon. She has to know the truth. She has to understand.

I decide to tell her the whole experience without insisting it was real. I'm certain she'll presume it was a dream.

She was quite entertained and moved by it, and I got a great deal of pleasure from that. She didn't question me at all about where the concept came from, which I found very odd.

I then ask her if she thinks it was real, and she gives me the most surprising answer.

"Of course it's real," she says. "You experienced it, and it changed you. Therefore it is real."

Yes, I think that is all that needs to be said.